A Bit of Me
A Bit of You
In My Arms Tonight
Where There's A Will
My Heart to Keep

Leopard's Spots

Levi
Oscar
Timothy
Isaiah
Gilbert
Esau
Sullivan
Wesley
Nischal
Justice
Sabin
Cliff

Mossy Glenn Ranch

Chaps and Hope
Ropes and Dreams
Saddles and Memories
Fences and Freedom
Riding and Regrets
Broncs and Bullies
Hay and Heartbreak
Vaqueros and Vigilance

Spotless

Hide
Hunt
Home
Heart

Coyote's Call

Off Course
In from the Cold
Blue Moon Rising

Valen's Pack

Run with the Moon
Exodus

The Vamp for Me

My Life Without Garlic
Don't Stake My Life on It
Sunshine is Overrated
Don't Drink the Holy Water
The Trouble with Mirrors
That's One Cross Vamp

City Shifters

Bearly There

Yes, Forever

Yes, Forever: Part One
Yes, Forever: Part Two
Yes, Forever: Part Three
Yes, Forever: Part Four
Yes, Forever: Part Five

What's His Passion?

Unexpected Places
Unexpected Moments

The Trouble with Mirrors

ISBN # 978-1-78651-372-4

©Copyright Bailey Bradford 2016

Cover Art by Posh Gosh ©Copyright 2016

Interior text design by Claire Siemaszkiewicz

Pride Publishing

Published in 2016 by Pride Publishing, Newland House, The Point, Weaver Road, Lincoln, LN6 3QN, United Kingdom.

Pride Publishing is a subsidiary of Totally Entwined Group Limited.

The Vamp for Me

THE TROUBLE WITH MIRRORS

BAILEY BRADFORD

Dedication

To my Hubs, who has made the past twenty-two years so
amazing.

Chapter One

The gold shorts were maybe too much. Paolo glanced over his shoulder and tried to look down at his ass. It really sucked not to be able to see himself in the mirror. Granted, the shorts would show up. It was just him, and those like him, that didn't have reflections.

"Definitely the worst thing about being a vamp," Paolo muttered, giving up on seeing his butt. It was there—he knew that much—but the overall effect of those shorts on his rump was beyond his ability to observe. He'd just have to hope his butt looked delicious. Or at least distracting—in a good way.

Paolo had very little body hair, just a smattering on his chest right between his nipples. It didn't even form a trail down to his pubes, instead completely vanishing until right below his belly button. His armpits and legs were sparsely covered, too, and his butt had only the lightest dusting of fuzz over it. Most of the time, he liked that he wasn't a bear—he was, thanks to the fact that he'd been turned on his twentieth birthday, a timeless twink.

Paolo snickered and slapped his butt cheeks. They were firm at least, and if he didn't have the best ass in existence, he certainly didn't have the worst, either—and *his* rump was real, honed and shaped by a lifetime of running and climbing mountains and hills in his native country. He'd been in peak shape when he'd been approached by what—who—he'd thought was an ancient god long ago.

Thinking about his past was a waste of time. Paolo ran a hand over his cock, then his balls, all barely covered by the shorts. He could almost make out the slit on top of his dick through the thin material. He grinned and figured he'd do well enough tonight at the club. He didn't even feel nervous about going, which was good. It'd taken him a few years to get past being attacked by vampire slayers in a dingy club—the same one he was returning to tonight.

Paolo tugged on a gold mesh shirt. He settled it so that his nipples were sticking out through two of the holes in it.

"Very nice, Paolo," said a man with a very cultured voice. One Paolo knew quite well.

"Claude." Paolo hadn't heard his coven leader enter the room—no surprise, considering Claude was freaky-sneaky and all-powerful, or just about all-powerful. "Is this good?" Paolo gestured to his clothes. "Or is it *too* good?"

Claude looked him over slowly, then frowned. "Abernathy, Radney, your opinions, please?"

"Too much?" Paolo started worrying immediately. He'd been joking about it being too good, but maybe it was. Perhaps more clothes were in order. He wanted to please his coven leader, but he also wanted to look sexy and maybe, just possibly, get laid. It'd been a while, way too long for a guy like him to go without. "I still have to put my boots on."

He crossed over to his dressing table and sat down. His white and gold ankle boots bordered on gaudy, but he loved the hell out of them. Paolo slipped them on and sighed. They were made of the softest Italian leather, and he would have worn them nonstop had they been practical. Part of the fun of wearing them was how impractical they were, however—the heels were spiked and a solid four inches high. It'd taken him a month to learn to walk in them without face-planting.

Paolo stood and struck a pose, left hip jutted, one leg out, other knee bent, head back, nose up, arms spread and hands up—almost jazz hands, but not that tacky. "How do I look?"

"Slay," Radney said.

No one else spoke.

Paolo lowered his head to find Abernathy and Claude looking at Radney like he was nuts.

Radney blushed and shrugged. "What? I thought that's what the cool kids said now. Paolo's slaying that look. If I weren't mated to my amazing…mate…I'd be all over him." Radney huffed. "Well, you know what I mean. Paolo looks like walking sex. Sex on legs. Er. That's a good thing, isn't it?"

Claude tutted and turned his attention back to Paolo. "Not necessarily. I merely want you to spy on the new slayers to be, not seduce them. Although… Perhaps that might not be a bad thing. However, that did not work so well for you before."

Paolo shuddered. "Yeah, well that was an accident. And also, no way, not even for you, Claude, and I have mad love for you." Fucking a vamp slayer was about as appealing as trying to get a suntan — *not happening*. "They might not even show up at the club. I mean, Erin could be wrong."

"Andrew said Erin is positive that he heard right," Radney responded, glancing at Claude then Paolo. "He was there at the table next to the Dark Slayers' group. They have three new members, and most of the Slayers are going to Violet Vines since it's a mix of LGBTQ and straight people who go there. Everyone in the Slayers should be there, celebrate the new members being brought in, and he suspects it's an initiation ceremony of some sorts, judging by what he overheard after the newbies left the table."

"And what did he overhear then?" Paolo asked, though he'd been told before. He just liked clarification.

Radney rolled his eyes. "Geez, Paolo. I *told* you. He heard the big ugly dude who leads the Slayers say they were going to initiate the newbs and if they were worth shit, they'd survive."

"Ah. We could just leave them to that dubious fate," Paolo pointed out. "And I could go dancing for the fun of it."

The Dark Slayers were idiots, and had the morals of a… *Well, something without morals.* They turned on their own and had killed members on occasion, though in the past few years, since the Dark Slayers had moved their headquarters to Vegas, Claude had been keeping a very close watch on them. He'd found more than one instance where he suspected murder within the Dark Slayers' ranks. Paolo tended not to ask for details, but now he wondered if he shouldn't have been so uninterested in the threats to the coven.

Claude touched Paolo's shoulder and Paolo shivered, his cock growing hard. He didn't worry about Abernathy or Claude taking offense. The reaction was purely instinctive, a primitive response to the most powerful vampire in existence. Paolo wanted to please his coven leader, and showing that he found Claude desirable wasn't an insult. Acting on it, now *that* was another matter. Abernathy would have Paolo's balls if Paolo tried to seduce Claude. Besides that, Claude only had eyes for his mate, which was as it should be. Regardless, that still didn't mean Paolo didn't get horny if Claude touched him, especially since it'd been *ages* since Paolo had gotten laid.

Claude's understanding look only made Paolo's shaft harder. He *really* needed to get laid.

"Paolo, you said you've been bored and restless, which is why I asked you to do this, but you can say no, even now. You can simply go out and find someone, or a few someones, to help you with that." Claude nodded toward Paolo's bulging cock. "There is also the dating website. It has been getting quite a few human applicants."

Paolo glanced down at it and gave his dick a light thump. "That thing needs to behave. I'm not interested in finding a mate online. Call me old-fashioned, but I want that to happen when Fate deems it time. Tonight, I want to help. The Dark Slayers are creepy, and even though you put the ones that knew about us in thrall and erased their memories of our encounter, the fact that they've made their headquarters here is" — Paolo struggled to find the right word, but there was only one that always came to him in regards to the Slayers—"creepy."

"Indeed," Claude murmured, taking a step back. "I have wondered about that myself, but in the years since they have settled here, we've not been approached or stalked a single time."

"Maybe they just like Vegas," Abernathy said, shrugging. "It's possible. There are plenty of vices here for psychos like them. Not that I'm saying people who live in Vegas are psychos, too. Just the Slayers. They can get away with a lot more here than other places, I think."

"Maybe," Claude agreed. "Regardless, I can't decide if it's better to have them here so we can keep an eye on them, or if I should encourage them to leave the area entirely. I'm growing tired of waiting for the Dark Slayers to cause trouble."

"Eh, let's wait and see what Paolo and Jude find out tonight," Abernathy suggested.

"Jude's coming with me?" Paolo asked. The newest member of the coven had come to them by way of Canada, in a roundabout manner. Jude been born in Ontario but wanted to come to the States for college, which was why he had been attending a university in Washington for a year. That's when he'd been turned by an unknown vampire. Jude probably wished to hell and back he'd never left Canada, and Claude had yet to discover the audacious vamp who'd turned Jude. It was a worrisome event.

"Yes, he is," Claude replied. "Jude's ready to start stepping out, so to speak."

Paolo nodded. Jude had spent most of his months with the coven keeping to himself. If he slipped out for blood, Paolo hadn't heard about it, so he assumed someone was bringing it in for him.

"Cool, okay. He's gonna be all right going with me, and going to a club?" Paolo ran a hand down his chest, trying his best not to let his sudden nervousness show. He didn't want Jude to hate him. Paolo liked to be liked.

"He's fine with it." Claude held one hand out to Abernathy.

"I think you will find Jude a most...suitable escort tonight." The wicked smile Claude flashed him was probably some kind of warning.

Paolo hoped it was. He needed some excitement in his life.

Chapter Two

"Jeeeeesus Christ," Paolo muttered, feeling his eyes bulge as he gawked at Jude. Unlike Paolo, Jude was tall, thickly muscled, and very masculine. *He even has hair on the backs of his knuckles!* And his chest was a damned pelt, that was all there was to it. Paolo poked the thick hair not covered by the black leather vest Jude was wearing. "I mean, holy shit, did you kill a beaver and decide to wear it?"

"A beaver?" Jude surprised him with a full-bodied laugh.

Paolo winced. "Well, look. I don't get the word beaver being equated to a vagina, okay? As far as I know, pussies don't have teeth, flat tails, and... If you keep laughing at me, I'll be forced to see how much of your chest hair I can rip out in one go."

Jude snorted, his ocean-green eyes watery from his amusement. He wiped at them. "Sorry, man. I haven't laughed in too long. I think all the repressed humor built up and overflowed."

The laughter seemed completely contrary to Jude's behavior up until then. Paolo couldn't let that go. "Why're you all happy now after you spent the last, what? Ten months or so hiding in your room?"

Jude's expression shifted from happy to shuttered in an instant. "Not everyone can take being turned into a monster with a grain of salt."

"We're not monsters," Paolo argued, folding his arms over his chest. "Look at me. I'm adorable, not something out of a horror movie, so cut out the monster crap. We're people, just a little different, but still people. We have feelings and shit too."

"Shit?" Jude arched one eyebrow at him.

Paolo rolled his eyes in return. "You know I didn't mean shit literally."

"Just thought I should check. You could be an exception to the rule that we don't need to do that," Jude said. "Or you could be full of it."

"Ha ha, you're a comedian." Paolo recognized a deflection when he heard one, and he let the whole subject drop. He wasn't a monster, though. No one would ever convince him otherwise. Paolo had a soul and morals, he had hopes and dreams. None of which he'd share with Jude unless they became really good friends.

"Well, let's get going. Are you driving or am I?" Paolo asked, striding toward the front door.

"Be careful," Claude called out from the office. "Do *not* put yourselves at risk."

"Aren't they kind of doing that just by going where the Slayers are?" Radney asked, scowling at Paolo. "We could go, me and Andrew—"

"No, Erin's coming to visit tonight," Paolo interrupted. "Stay here. I'm sure me and Jude can handle a little spying."

"They'll be fine, Radney." Claude walked out of the office and nodded at Paolo and Jude. "Paolo is smart and adept at surviving. Jude is…" Claude looked at the newest vamp and smirked just a tiny bit. "Huge. I don't think anyone will mess with him or Paolo."

"Yeah, we'll be fine. Later, dude." Paolo opened the door and darted outside. The moonlight streaked the desert with silver, and some of the sand gleamed like it was made from chips of diamonds. The sky was all but cloudless, and it was, of course, hot as hell. There wasn't even a breeze to offset the heat. "Gotta love the desert in August."

"I don't." Jude pulled his long brown hair into a ponytail. "And to answer your question from inside, I'm driving the buggy for now."

Paolo didn't ask what the 'for now' meant. He just got on and when Jude was seated in front of him, tried to wrap his arms around Jude. The man was too muscled for Paolo's fingers to touch. "You're huge."

"All over," Jude agreed before starting the dune buggy.

That stopped the conversation for the length of the drive. When they reached the designated spot to stash the buggy, a small duo of buildings owned by the coven for just such a purpose, Jude cut the engine and they both dismounted.

"Now what?" Paolo asked.

"Now, that," Jude replied, pointing at something behind Paolo.

Paolo turned and it was then that he saw the chrome and black motorcycle.

"Of *course* you drive a motorcycle, you big, bad, testosterone-infused man," Paolo said not quite under his breath.

"Have to compensate somehow," Jude informed him.

Paolo glanced at Jude's groin. Unless Jude padded that area, he had absolutely nothing to compensate for. Which meant, he supposed, that Jude was joking, or he was modest. Paolo didn't know him well enough to guess which.

"Ready?" Jude trotted over to the motorcycle. He got on with an ease Paolo envied. "Or are you scared of riding one of these?"

Paolo laughed and joined him at the bike. His first attempt to get on almost resulted in him tripping, but he managed to get his leg over the seat and to slide on behind Jude. "Show me what you've got, stud."

Jude started the motorcycle, then they were off. The night air was hot, but Paolo was used to it. He'd lived in the desert for so long, he easily imagined he had sand in his veins. The stars were bright and numerous overhead, a blur as he looked up.

The faster they went, the lighter Paolo felt, the happier he was, as if they were able to outrun his worries and stress.

What did he have to worry and stress over anyway? He asked himself that but found no answer. He was an apex predator—albeit not *the* apex predator in their coven, that title belonged to Claude—and he could, possibly, live forever as long as he avoided sunlight, holy water, garlic, stakes through the heart, beheading... Well, he could live a lot longer than any human, at any rate, as long as he was careful.

He had friends at the coven, and people he cared about.

But it wasn't enough.

And he wasn't being careful, riding on the back of a motorcycle with a new coven member who probably wasn't stable upstairs. *Going on a spy mission to infiltrate the vermin that want us dead...* It was possible he was being a *tad* melodramatic.

It was better than trying to figure out why he'd felt so weird lately. Introspection gave him a headache.

Getting laid would make him feel better. Maybe he'd get a nibble or two, too. Suck a little blood, a little cock— *Not a little cock. I want a jaw-stretcher.* Paolo grinned and stopped thinking about anything other than the amazing vibrations to his balls and cock from the big motorcycle. It was like riding a giant sex toy. Paolo approved, definitely.

All the way to the club, he imagined different scenarios for how the sex would go down later, once he'd finished his spy business. He was leaning toward getting fucked— the bike really *was* making him hornier than a three-horned Billy goat.

A blow job would be great, too, or even a hand job for that matter. He just wanted to get off with someone else, and wow, did that realization make him feel like a lonely little loser.

Paolo gave himself a mental smack. He wasn't a moody little twit—he was fun and outgoing and it'd just been too long since he'd been sociable outside the coven.

That was all it was, the whole reason he felt so off center.

And he could fix the issue, just as soon as he made sure the Slayers weren't going to be causing any trouble.

Chapter Three

Getting dragged to a club with a bunch of weirdos was definitely one of Dakota Dickens' ideas of hell. He had several, being the unsociable asshole that he was—his brother's words.

Hanging out with his brother Utah Owens, and Utah's best friend, Kellan, and the nuts who called themselves the Dark Slayers, was definitely hell. Dakota didn't know Kellan very well, but even if he did, it wouldn't have mattered.

Clubbing or bar-hopping was something Dakota just didn't do.

Usually. But if he wanted a chance to get out of poverty…

Even so, Dakota wished to high heaven he'd never come to Nevada, that things were different and he was still living in his nice apartment in Minnesota.

Okay, not a nice *apartment, but still. I wouldn't be here with the loonies. Stupid me. Stupid broken heart. Stupid family. Stupid will.*

Out of those four stupids, Dakota focused only on one—family. He'd come to Vegas looking for his brother, and now he was in a mess. He cut his half-brother an annoyed look as Utah laughed and slapped Kellan on the back. Whatever they were talking about, Dakota wanted no part of.

Once again, he wondered if Utah had been lying. Utah had kind of implied that if Dakota didn't join his stupid, crazy, delusional vampire hunter cult, Dakota would end up dead. Between that and the will, he had felt he had no choice but to go along with Utah, at least until Dakota could find a way to get his inheritance and get out of Nevada. And forget that he had any family left. *I was so damned happy to find out I have half- brothers...* Well, sometimes ignorance really *was* bliss.

The music coming from the club could be heard a block away. Dakota winced. He couldn't dance worth shit. He was about as coordinated as a marionette with each of its strings tied to a different goat in a stampede. He was *that* bad.

Plus, he hated crowds. Bars. *People. Ugh! Why didn't I remember that* before *I hunted down my brother?* Right, because he'd had to come find Utah, as that damn will had directed him to do. *Led like a sheep to the slaughter.*

For someone who was supposed to be smart, he was pretty stupid sometimes.

He'd been lonely, though, as well as totally broke. Apparently that combo resulted in him making poor decisions. Hence his current predicament.

Utah looked back over his shoulder at Dakota. "Come on, Dak! Smile! At least we're doing this at a place that's got gays in it, too. We coulda gone to a solid straight bar instead."

Dakota refrained from pointing out it would have sucked no matter what kind of club or bar they took him to. And he really didn't want a stupid tattoo, either, but again, Utah had implied it was that, and this initiation tonight, or death—because, according to him, no one could know about the Dark Slayers and live unless they were one of the Dark Slayers.

It all sounded like a ridiculously tacky horror novel in the making. All the over-testosteroned men, thumping their chests and stomping their feet before they gathered up pitchforks and torches to go after the evil Count Dracula. To Dakota, they were just boys who refused to grow up, and who'd made their own idiotic little club since no legitimate club would have let them in.

Not that he could tell Utah that. Dakota was afraid Utah would go right to Ernest, the leader of the delusional Slayers. Just because Dakota thought their group was a load of bullshit didn't mean the members of it weren't fully invested. He was fairly certain everyone he'd met in the Slayers had not only drunk the Kool-Aid, as the saying went, but bathed in it and possibly snorted it, too. He was surrounded by unstable maniacs, and they all carried sharp stakes and vials of holy water.

Living on the streets really might be preferable. Being completely broke might be, too.

Damn it, he *really* didn't want a tattoo.

"Come on! Maybe you can finally get laid," Utah urged. "I bet the others are already here."

Dakota blinked away his mental bitching and found that Utah and Kellan were almost to the club doors. A line of about a dozen people were waiting to be let in.

"I told you, I'm going to remain celibate the rest of my life," Dakota muttered.

Utah laughed—just like he had every time Dakota said that—and slapped him on the back, hard enough to make Dakota stumble. *Just like he always does.*

"You don't mean that," Utah was saying, a smarmy grin on his face. "Sex is awesome! No one gives up sex. All those people going on about being asexual just haven't had a decent—"

"Can you not?" Dakota interrupted, wincing at his brother's obnoxiousness.

Utah shrugged and leaned close. "Whatevs, bro. I'm going to get a blow job, at least. All these almost-naked women and the gay guys love blowing guys like me," he whispered right into Dakota's ear.

Dakota recoiled and felt the sneer trying to curl his top lip. It took a lot of effort, but he repressed it and settled for shaking his head in disgust. "No, that's *so* not true."

Kellan bobbed his head. "Dak's right, Ute. That'd be like saying he wants to suck mine just 'cause I'm straight."

Utah smacked Kellan on the arm. "Don't be gross! That's my little brother you're talking about!"

Dakota didn't bother to point out that he was hardly an

innocent little boy, and hadn't even known Utah existed until a month ago.

"Do you have a thing for Dak?" Utah asked of Kellan in a demanding tone. "You said you were into women."

Kellan flinched, a subtle twitch around the eyes and mouth that Dakota saw, but wasn't sure if Utah caught. "I am," Kellan said a second later, holding his hands up as if to stop Utah's accusations manually. "I was just making a point. Those guys and women in there and in line are someone's brothers or sons, sisters or daughters. Someone probably loves them. Think about that."

Dakota was beyond surprised by the surprisingly deep observation from Kellan. Normally the guy came off like he'd just stepped out of a cave. And maybe Dakota was guilty of thinking of Kellan as a Neanderthal, but he wasn't changing his mind just because the guy said something decent for once.

"Yeah," Utah drawled, "and all the women I fuck are someone's—" He stopped and grimaced. "God damn it, why'd you have to say that? Now I'm gonna feel guilty every time I get laid."

"Is that going to stop you from having sex?" Dakota asked, knowing the answer even as he spoke.

Utah snorted and rolled his eyes. "Yeah, right. Nope. And if I get drunk enough tonight, I won't even remember this conversation, so that's the plan. We'll get drunk, get you laid, then get the tattoo done and you'll be ready for the ceremony. It'll be great. Come on."

Dakota had just opened up his mouth to argue when glittery movement to his left caught his attention. He turned his head, and his heart fluttered when he saw the sexy little guy in the mesh shirt, gold shorts and matching ankle boots.

Although... He sure didn't look so little down south. Dakota tried not to be obvious in his ogling, but *damn!* He'd always had a thing for guys substantially shorter than him, and different from him, period. He was such an introvert that he needed someone more outgoing as a partner.

Not that he was thinking along those lines in regards to Goldie. Not at all. He was just admiring the man. He was so sexy. Dakota wanted to touch his thick black hair and—

"Let's get in line."

Dakota jolted upon hearing his brother's voice. He'd forgotten all about Utah and Kellan. "Yeah, okay." He dragged his gaze away from Goldie, catching the flash of white teeth as the stranger smiled at him. *Oops. Busted.* That smile was devastating. Dakota couldn't look away as he followed Utah and Kellan, keeping them in his peripheral vision as he gave up and just flat-out stared like the rude asshole he'd suddenly become.

Goldie didn't seem to mind, winking at him and smiling again.

Dakota wished the sun was still out. He wanted a better look at Goldie, wanted so see if his eyes were dark brown or black, if his lashes were as thick as they appeared to be, whether his lips were as full as they looked or if he'd somehow made them up to appear that way. Goldie's bronze skin had to be soft to the touch. Dakota didn't know why he thought that, but he did, and he had to clench his hands into fists to keep from reaching toward Goldie when they ended up in line behind him.

Utah nudged Dakota to the front of their trio. Utah leaned close and Dakota prepared himself for more ludicrous whispers from his brother. "Look at that guy in the gold shorts. He's got an ass that most girls would envy."

Well, maybe not so ludicrous, though Dakota didn't think envying Goldie's ass was limited to one gender.

Goldie turned around and looked at Dakota, letting his gaze linger at Dakota's groin.

Dakota's dick obviously wasn't interested in his vow of celibacy. It began to grow erect under Goldie's gaze.

Dakota started to put his hands in front of his cock, then realized how absurd he was being. Which left him with his hands about waist-high, looking like a moron. He quickly tucked his thumbs in the front pockets of his Levi's. There was a way to place his hands that would frame his burgeoning erection, but Dakota was damned if he could think how to do it.

And what was he doing ogling Goldie anyway? Dakota cringed. He was such an idiot. Goldie was dressed to party, and he was sexy as fuck, whereas Dakota was tall and scrawny and wearing jeans and a concert T-shirt. He wasn't even close to being as handsome as Goldie, who was, honestly, stunning. Dakota had always had a thing for men with dark hair.

"See something you like, Dakota?" Utah asked, nudging Dakota's back. "Is he your type?"

Dakota cringed. Utah hadn't bothered to keep his voice down, and Goldie *had* to have heard him.

Before Dakota could so much as turn away, Goldie licked his lips.

Dakota was entranced by the glide of that pink tongue over plush lips. The street light reflected off the wet skin and reminded Dakota of blow jobs and kissing, two of his very favorite things in the world.

He felt dizzy, and realized as his chest started to ache, that he hadn't bothered to breathe. He inhaled sharply, and raised his gaze a little higher, just in time to see Goldie wink at him.

Did that mean he had a chance with the sexy man? Dakota couldn't tell if that had been flirty or sarcastic. Mocking. Something not kind to him. Reading people was not his strong suit. It was why he had a broken heart and no money—

Except his heart didn't feel so broken anymore. In the past few months, the emotional wound he'd thought was too deep to heal, and the constant pain of loss he'd first felt after being dumped, seemed to have faded to an itchy scar.

Or maybe he was just *really* horny. Dakota hadn't had a great number of sexual partners—two, including his own hand—so that might be why he wasn't missing James so much...or at all.

Goldie looked him over one more time, then turned around as the line moved forward.

Dakota nearly tripped over his tongue as he viewed the man from the back. More specifically, as he ogled the very nice round, plump butt that was barely covered by the gold shorts. He'd checked it out before, but he was closer now, and the urge to cup that ass in his hands was almost irresistible. If Dakota had been the forward and daring kind, he'd have done it, just put his hands over those tempting cheeks. Even thinking about it made his dick harden.

Goldie looked back over his shoulder at Dakota and there was no mistaking the lust in his expression. Even Dakota couldn't miss it, and his heartbeat doubled as he flushed with warmth.

"Looks like a sure thing," Utah said. "Go for it, bro."

Dakota wasn't sure how he was supposed to go for it, but he was going to do his damnedest to figure it out. If he could work up the nerve—and if he didn't get trapped into talking with the Slayers all night.

As if him thinking about them somehow made them appear, Dakota caught sight of several men strolling down the sidewalk toward the club. He kept his groan to a mental one. If he was smart enough, he would find a way to ditch them all.

Maybe the money wasn't worth whatever weird things they wanted to make him do.

But he'd need to start by getting some breathing room, and if he could swing it, some alone time with Goldie. Because if he was going to dream, he was damn sure going to dream big, and Goldie was the biggest treasure he'd seen in a long time.

Dakota turned to Utah. "You know, if you really want me to get laid, maybe you and Kellan should meet up with the other guys and leave me in line here. Give me time to work my charm?"

"You have charm?" Utah asked. He looked doubtful.

"Are you sure about that? Or did you read some book with lame pick-up advice?"

"Ute, maybe we should give him some space to maneuver in," Kellan said quietly, his gaze locking onto Dakota's.

Dakota couldn't help but feel that Kellan knew how much he hated all the Slayer bullshit. That couldn't have been right, though, because Kellan was helping him out now. If he suspected Dakota wasn't loyal to the Slayers, he wouldn't do that. *Would he?*

"We *are* kind of tough competition for him," Utah said after a moment. "Fine. Let's meet Ernest and the others. They have the rest of the newbs with them, right?"

"Yeah, I think so." Kellan gave the barest nod, then he used a hand on Utah's shoulder to guide him away.

Dakota breathed a sigh of relief. He hoped Goldie hadn't overheard anything, but since Goldie was currently chatting away with two women, he suspected the conversation between Utah, Kellan and himself had gone unnoticed.

Now, if he could only manage to snag Goldie's interest…

Chapter Four

Jude was keeping his distance from Paolo, which was a good idea. No one would want to have sex with Paolo if they thought he was with Jude. They'd fear for their lives. The man had a scowl that could curdle milk and turn holy water hellish. But he seemed like a nice enough guy, to Paolo at least.

Even so, they'd decided to split up. Jude would stay closer to the Slayers once they'd all gathered at the club, and Paolo would cull his prey.

That prey happened to be right behind him. The tall, thin guy in the ill-fitting jeans was cute. Paolo couldn't figure out just what it was about the man that caught his attention, but something did — something other than the obvious.

Which, considering he was with the two members of the Dark Slayers, worked out nicely in some ways. Thanks to Claude's dossier on the Slayers, Paolo pretty much recognized the regular members. The newbies, not by photos, but he'd read the names.

Dakota. Paolo had also just heard his name, and seriously doubted there were two guys named Dakota out at the club tonight. Despite him telling Claude he wouldn't have sex with a Slayer, Paolo was attracted to Dakota. There was a lost look about him, and he didn't seem thrilled to be at the club. It made Paolo think maybe he wasn't too keen on being a Slayer.

Even so, that meant Dakota was still off the potential fuck list. But Paolo could have some fun.

Lucky me. Paolo all but rubbed his hands together and cackled in glee. He was going to get laid, and he'd get to wind up a would-be Slayer, too. Two different things, because no way was he having sex with any idiot wanting to join the Dark Slayers. Which meant he'd be teasing Dakota as much as he could before he found someone he *could* have sex with. And in all the teasing, he'd hope to find out what the Dark Slayers were up to. It seemed, so far, that the thrall Claude had cast over the Dark Slayers years back was still holding up — as it should. Claude was no one to be fucked with. He could scramble someone's brains with a snap of his fingers when he put them in thrall.

Although Paolo knew of two humans who'd broken Claude's thrall, so there was that. One of those humans was now Radney's mate, Andrew, and the other was Andrew's twin brother, Erin.

Paolo had kind of had a *thing* for Erin there for a while, but he'd gotten past it. The desire to settle down with a mate had been pressing on him at the time, what with Radney, Claude and Tony all having found their mates. Of course there were other mated vamps, but Paolo didn't really talk with most of them.

Anyway, he was over wanting a mate of his own. Now he just wanted sex. Preferably with someone good at it. There had been a few duds in that area in Paolo's past.

He glanced behind him again, and grinned when he caught Dakota staring at his ass. At least he was pretty sure that was where Dakota was looking. Paolo wiggled it and was rewarded with a gasp from Dakota. Paolo faced away, not really seeing the people in front of him as he thought about Dakota.

This is too much fun. I bet he'd be a great fuck. He looks at me like he wants to just...devour me, and not in the creepy, ax-wielding sociopath kind of way. Paolo was desperate for someone to really *see* him, though he hated to admit it. Dakota was definitely seeing him, and it was arousing enough that Paolo was going to end up with his dick poking out the top of his shorts if he didn't get a grip on himself.

It was kind of shitty that Dakota was the enemy. Paolo

wasn't horny enough to cross that line. He let himself fantasize about finding out Dakota was innocent of hanging with the Slayers willingly, that they held him prisoner and were forcing him to join their stupid ranks, and Paolo could rescue him from that fate.

"Five bucks."

Paolo blinked and realized he was at the entrance of the club. He hadn't even paid attention to the fact that he was moving along in the line.

He took a five from the waistband of his shorts. "Sure thing, stud." The bouncer was huge and so not Paolo's type, but it never hurt to flirt. He grinned brightly as the bouncer looked him over.

"Sweet," the bouncer said. "Go in."

"Oh, I hear that *all* the time, and if someone's special enough, I make that offer, too." Paolo blew him a kiss and risked another glance back to find Dakota frowning.

Paolo barely repressed a grin. It seemed to him that Dakota didn't like him flirting with the big man at the door.

Rather than dwell on it, Paolo stepped into the club and was immediately assailed with strong, sometimes rancid scents — sweat, sex, need, booze and blood, so much blood. All of it was contained in human veins, however, and none had been spilled. His vamp senses detected the availability of food and the possibility of threats. He could hear, see and smell better than any human. That usually came in handy, but when he was in a loud, odiferous place, it could be less...helpful.

Paolo wrinkled his nose and snorted, as if he could clear the stench from his nostrils. He moved deeper into the club, ignoring the strobe lights overhead and cringing at the awful dance music being played. The DJ must have been new or tone deaf. Or both.

The floor was sticky, his shoes getting a light tug every time he took a step, like the flooring was trying to keep his foot down.

The club itself was crowded, and more than once, Paolo

was groped as he made his way closer to the dance floor. The second he reached the writhing, dancing mass of bodies, Paolo slipped right in and closed his eyes as he began to dance.

Soon, sweat coated his skin—other men's, not his, as he didn't perspire anymore—but the scent of it was very arousing. It reminded him of his mortal past, when he used to run and fuck and fight as a man. Now he was still that same man in some ways, but in others, that old him had died the night he'd been turned.

Paolo didn't want to think about the past. He let the music carry him, felt it thrumming through his veins, his heart pounding with the heavy bass. Even with his eyes closed, he kept seeing flashes of light, the strobes going strong overhead.

Someone was behind him, grinding hard against his ass. A few other people were around Paolo, one in front of him, some on the sides.

Paolo's cock was hard, though he wasn't about to get off. He just reveled in dancing and feeling men so close, let their scents feed the slow-building hunger in his gut. He'd fed before coming out tonight, so he wasn't in danger of losing control and biting someone, but that didn't mean the vamp part of him could ignore all the yummy blood types he detected.

After a while, and several subtle and not so subtle rejections to some of his dance partners, Paolo reminded himself that he was there for a task, not just fun. He figured he'd given the Slayers enough time to have a few drinks, which would make them sloppy and easier to get information out of.

Several of them were there now, taking up a half dozen tables to the left of the dance floor. Jude was lurking in the shadows behind them, talking to a twink who bounced around like he was a tweaker.

Paolo quickly put names to bodies, biting back a grimace when he looked at Ernest. That man was uglier than a turd dropped in mud. Someone had beaten him not with an ugly stick, but with the whole species of the plant. If such a plant existed. Paolo averted his gaze.

He'd go for the weakest link, which probably wouldn't be the big guy sitting across from Dakota. Kellan, Paolo would be willing to bet, because the third man looked like Dakota, somewhat. That had to be Utah. Once again, Paolo was glad he'd been given some intel, though he supposed it wasn't necessary. Both Utah and Kellan, as well as the other Slayers, wore tank tops that showed off part of their Slayer tattoo.

Paolo ordered a drink at the bar and studied his targets. He frowned, narrowing his eyes as he looked at Kellan's tattoo. There was something...off about it. Paolo couldn't put his finger on it, then he quit trying because Dakota stood up and started walking his way.

This is interesting. Dakota kept watching him, never once glancing away as he strode toward Paolo.

Paolo heard Utah and a few other idiots cheer, "Go get you some, Dak!"

Dakota cringed and his face turned pink with a blush, but he didn't stop or falter in his approach.

Paolo set his drink down. It'd been nothing more than a prop anyway. He turned, putting his back to the bar, resting his elbows on it and jutting his pelvis out. The pose put his dick on display, and Paolo was rewarded then with a stumble by Dakota before he closed the last of the distance between them.

Paolo arched one eyebrow at Dakota, waiting for him to speak.

Dakota's mouth moved, but not words came out at first. Then there was a squeak that made Dakota blush an even deeper shade of pink before he managed, "Hi."

Paolo grinned. "Hi. You got a name, sugar?"

Dakota gulped, his Adam's apple bobbing rapidly. "Y-yeah, I... Uh. Dakota. Dakota Dickens."

Paolo tried to stop himself, he really did, but he giggled anyway. "Dickens? Really? How convenient. I totally approve of that as a last name for a gay man."

"Thanks? I guess?" Dakota didn't sound very certain as he wiped at his forehead with one hand. "I... I don't really know what to do here. What's your name?"

Dakota seemed charmingly clueless. Not like a psycho-vampire slayer at all. Paolo held out his right hand to Dakota. "Paolo." *Whoops. Should have used a fake name. Damn it.* Usually he was smarter than that. Then again, as far as he knew, none of the Slayers knew there were really vampires in Vegas, so his name shouldn't give anything away.

When Dakota shook his hand, Paolo was surprised by the firm grip. "Nice," he praised, giving Dakota's hand a squeeze, and not letting it go. "You've got a good grip, sugar."

"Dad insisted I have a good handshake," Dakota said. "One of the few things I remember about him." Then he huffed and rolled his eyes. "Sorry, that's not the kind of thing we're supposed to talk about."

Paolo stood straight. "What *are* we supposed to talk about?"

Dakota gulped again, and a series of *uhs* came out of his mouth as he tugged his hand from Paolo's grip. Dakota had deep green eyes, with flecks of gray and brown close to the irises. Thick, blond-tipped lashes framed his eyes, and Paolo thought that he could have stood there looking at them, at Dakota, for a long time before he'd discovered everything about his features. It was crazy. Paolo shouldn't feel attraction like what was building in him, not for an enemy in the making.

That reminder caused Paolo to shake himself mentally. *Get your shit together, idiot!* He smiled at Dakota. "Well?"

Dakota shrugged. "I—I don't know. I mean, you're not dressed for conversation, right?" Then he clapped a hand over his mouth. "Oh my God, I'm an asshole," he blurted, the words muffled somewhat but still discernible.

Paolo wondered if Dakota was really an asshole or just socially awkward. Then he wondered why it mattered. *Of* course *he's an asshole – he's joining the Dark Slayers.* "That was definitely an asshole kind of thing to say." Paolo tutted. "I'm disappointed. You looked like such a fun potential fuck." And that was true, even though he didn't want to screw around with a Slayer or Slayer to be.

Dakota lowered his hand from his mouth. "I know," he muttered. "I am *such* a jerk. I didn't mean it like you didn't deserve a conversation because of how you're dressed. That's awful. That's like saying a woman deserved to get raped because of how she was dressed. Jesus, what archaic misogyny. Wait, is it misogyny if I applied it to you?"

"And you think any of that is appropriate club convo with a stranger?" Paolo asked, tutting again. "Sugar, you need some help with picking up men. Maybe less talk and more flirting, like telling me how marvelous my ass looks in these shorts."

Dakota was blushing once again, but he nodded. "You do. I mean it does. I know. I suck at it. I'm sorry. This whole night is fucked up."

Paolo was strangely inclined to believe him. Whatever Dakota was, he wasn't a hardened, crazy Slayer. No one could act as innocent and awkward as him. "What're you doing here?" Paolo asked, glaring at a man who jostled him trying to get to the bar. "Watch it, dickface."

The man flipped him off.

"Wow, I'm wounded, and not even on my worst day, hon." Paolo turned his attention back to Dakota. "So?"

Dakota glanced behind him, toward the tables where a lot of the Slayers sat watching. "Well." He looked at Paolo. "I'm here with them, sort of, and it's really stupid. I don't think you want to hear about it. You'd think I'm crazy if I told you, anyway."

"Really," Paolo drawled, moving closer to Dakota and placing a hand on his arm. "That sounds intriguing. Why don't we find a table and sit down? You can tell me all about what brings you here tonight."

"It's so stupid, surely you don't want to hear about it. If I tell you, you'll walk off. No, you'll run," Dakota protested, but he allowed Paolo to lead him to a small table on the other side of the club.

They were out of sight of Utah and Kellan, which had been Paolo's goal, because now he was thinking, maybe, just *maybe*, Dakota wasn't a bad guy after all.

"Want a drink?" Paolo thought to ask before they sat down.

Dakota shook his head. "God, no. I had a couple beers already, and that's enough to make me tipsy."

"Tipsy, hm?" Paolo sat across from Dakota. "Just from two beers?"

"I don't drink, normally," Dakota said. "I don't like alcohol. Too many alcoholics in my family."

"Oh? There were a lot of them?" Paolo asked, folding his hands on top of the table.

"Well, just my mom," Dakota muttered. "She was all the family I had once Dad left. Then I found out I have some half-brothers...and there was the will, and —" He narrowed his eyes. "Though I'm thinking I'd have been better off not knowing any of that. Look where it got me."

"It got you here, with me," Paolo pointed out, grinning. "So maybe not such a bad thing?"

Dakota groaned and lowered his head to his hands on the tabletop. "Aw, no, man. You have *no* idea how crazy my brother Utah is. And his group of insane friends. They're like a cult of insanity. Jesus."

Paolo wavered. Maybe he was being played, after all. His little fantasy about Dakota being innocent, forced to partake in the Dark Slayers' crap, was too close to the truth, otherwise.

"You could leave, right?" Paolo waited while Dakota groaned again. "Just leave, sugar, if you're so miserable."

Dakota raised his head then, and his pretty green eyes seemed to gleam with unshed tears. "I don't have any money. James, my ex, took everything we had in the bank. Once I got here, I lost my wallet, and I don't have a car or anything. I just left, just came here after..." He winced.

"After what?" Paolo prodded, tempted to reach for Dakota's hands. He had an odd desire to comfort Dakota.

"After I found my boyfriend of two years fucking the neighbor in our bed." Dakota slumped down in the seat. "I was too boring. James needed more."

Paolo grimaced but quickly replaced it with a smile. "Sugar, James sounds like an asshole. If he was bored, he should have talked to you, not fucked the neighbor."

Dakota laughed, though the sound held bitterness rather than joy. "Yeah, or I shouldn't have been boring. Now I'm stuck in Vegas, about to be forced to get a tattoo I never wanted, and made to join a cult full of bloodthirsty, delusional fools."

"Why join them? Just say no," Paolo advised as the music swelled even louder.

Dakota cupped a hand to his ear, as if to signal he hadn't heard Paolo's question.

Paolo slid out of his seat, then moved to sit beside Dakota. "So why join them?" he repeated. "Say no."

"I can't," Dakota replied. He looked at Paolo then down at the table. "Utah—my brother—said they'd kill me if I don't join, because I know too much. *That's* how crazy they are. How delusional. Then there's the will, though the more I think about it, the less I want the money."

Paolo let the will part pass by. He had more immediate concerns. Had he been a regular human, he'd have thought Dakota was bat-shit crazy, but he was a vamp, and he knew for a fact he existed. Poor Dakota didn't have a clue, however. Paolo focused on the potential for fratricide. "Your own brother would kill you?" That was horrifying, but not exactly surprising. Dark Slayers were off the rails, as far as he was concerned.

Dakota rubbed his chin. "Well, I don't think *he'd* do it, but he might not stop the other Slayers from killing me. They are all pretty convinced there are vampires in the world, and apparently, our family—on our shared father's side—

have always been members of the Dark Slayers. God," Dakota groaned. "That name sounds like an old eighties rock band. The kind with the big hair and bad makeup."

"It does," Paolo agreed, his mind racing as he tried to decide what to do. "The one-hit wonder kind."

"I came here tonight because they made me," Dakota continued. "There's supposed to be an initiation later. Utah knows I hate the idea of getting a tattoo. It's just not for me, though I think they can be sexy on other people. So he figured, get me drunk and laid, and I'd be mellow enough not to fight about the tattoo or the rest of the initiation. The other new guys are all excited about the tatts and everything. I'm just...not."

"How many of you guys are getting tattoos? What's the rest of the initiation?" Paolo asked, leaning against Dakota just because he wanted to. He had more questions to ask but didn't want to come across as grilling Dakota too much. But one more would be okay. "Is it something bad?"

"Uh, two others besides me. One of the Slayers is supposed to do the tattoos. The other guys joining are some relatives of Ernest. I don't know what the rest of the initiation is," Dakota answered. "No one will tell me. All I know is that I'm supposed to get the tattoo, then be taken to some undisclosed spot and something else happens at that point. Then a week or so later, I'm officially made a member of the Dark Slayers. Insane, right?"

Well, it was something, that was for sure. Paolo wondered what the initiation was once the tattoo had been done.

"You probably think I'm making all this up," Dakota continued, running one hand along his jaw before tangling his fingers in his shoulder-length blond hair. "I'm not. There's money involved, too. Maybe not a lot to most people, and maybe not enough to me, anymore. Ten grand to follow my absentee-father's will? Which means going through with the Slayers shit. Why aren't you running yet?"

Paolo pursed his lips as he thought about his answer. He didn't want to come off as too blasé, but a regular human would likely think Dakota was a card shy of a full deck. "I've heard of stranger things. The Dark Slayers aren't exactly unknown in Vegas." Which was true. They never hid who or what they were, and had a recruiting website listing the address to their headquarters. "Ten grand is a lot, but is it worth being marked with a tattoo? It'd cost thousands to have that fucker removed with a laser, and I've heard it hurts way worse than getting the actual tattoo does." Maybe the fear of more pain would deter Dakota. "As for the Slayers, they aren't the only crazy cult in existence. There are all kinds of cults, and people who think they're vampires or some other kind of supernatural creature. Or pretend like they are." Paolo waved a hand. "I'm not sure which, or if it's both—whatever. The point is, I guess if there are people that believe they're vampires, there will probably be people who think they need to kill the vampires. People *always* find an excuse to kill, it seems. Not all people, but you know." Paolo gave a raspy chuckle. "They kill over religion, money, power—over stupid things and nothing at all."

Dakota sat back, his eyes wide. "Wow. That's kind of cynical."

"It's not cynical," Paolo protested. "It's the truth. You only have to look at human history to see it."

Dakota's mouth quirked up on one side. "I can't believe we're sitting in a place that smells like sex and desperation, and we're talking about mankind's propensity for offing people."

Paolo laughed. Dakota had a point—and Paolo was there to do a job, which was to gather information on the Dark Slayers. That reminder stripped away his amusement. "So, what're you going to do?"

"I don't know." Dakota glanced around. "I think Utah took my wallet and cell phone, though I haven't asked him. I mean, I just showed up at his door a month ago and introduced myself as his half-brother. I was glad he welcomed me without question. Surprised, too, until he told me he had the same letter from our father, naming me and a some other guys as all being dear old Dad's offspring and talking about what we had to do to inherit the money he'd left behind."

"Where are the others?" Paolo asked.

"No idea," Dakota replied with a shrug as he scraped one fingernail on the table, picking at the peeling paint. "I did a quick check online at a library when I snuck away once, but never found them. Utah doesn't have a computer." He grimaced as he looked at his fingernail. "We're all named after states. Utah. Dakota, Nevada, Washington. Don't know why. Me and Utah weren't born in the states we're named after. I'm guessing the other two weren't, either."

Paolo would make sure Claude knew there were more Slayers' sons out walking around in the world. He'd bet Claude would have Nevada and Washington tracked down in no time at all.

"Apparently, my father was some big-wig in the Slayers, not just a regular member." Dakota jolted like he'd been goosed. "You know, maybe I should have another beer. Or a shot of something stronger."

Paolo really liked the cut of Dakota's cheekbones, and the jut of his pointed chin. He liked just about everything about Dakota's appearance. He also thought that Dakota wasn't a willing Slayer-to-be, money aside.

Which meant Paolo was going to do something that Claude would probably brain him for later. Or at least scold him severely. Paolo was going to rescue a human.

Chapter Five

Dakota felt Paolo studying him, and fought not to twitch under the scrutiny. Somehow, what he'd been certain was going to be a horrible night was turning out...not so bad. Weird, yes, but he'd been told he was weird often enough. He had 'quirks' as James had called them at first. Odd behaviors that, while they harmed no one, weren't normal. Except they were normal for him, and maybe meeting a sexy guy at a club and having a deep conversation was just an extension of Dakota's oddness.

Or he was really lonely, and scared, and Paolo was being a nice guy.

"Is that ten grand really important to you?" Paolo asked.

Dakota thought about it for a few seconds. "No. If I'm honest, I'm not even sure there's money for me. I feel like I've been played ever since I got here — to Vegas, I mean."

"Come with me," Paolo finally said. "If you want to get away from what they're forcing you to do, then leave with me, right now. I wish I could offer you ten grand to compensate you, but I can't. I can just offer you a safe place to stay."

Dakota blinked then shook his head. "What do you mean?" Lord, he sounded dense.

"I mean, *come with me*," Paolo repeated, grabbing his hand and squeezing it. "Money isn't everything, sugar. It really isn't. Life, a good life, that's what matters. Get up, and we'll go to the back room like we're going to fuck. I'll get you out of here, and away from your brother and his, er, cult."

"But why?" Dakota asked a little desperately, striving to understand. Paolo was handsome, so sexy it made Dakota ache to look at him, and Dakota was just...him. "Oh." Dakota thought he got it then. "You're a nice guy, and you just want to help me. I can't let you —"

Paolo hissed. *Hissed!* For some reason, Dakota's dick flared back to life. It'd gone soft as he'd sat with Utah and Kellan, but now he could have used it to bat with.

"I want to fuck you," Paolo said bluntly. "But I want to help you, too. I can do both. If you really don't want to end up with a shitty tattoo and to be forced into the Slayers, I'm offering you a way out. Sex isn't mandatory, either. I'll help you even if you don't want me. Can't do anything about the money, though."

"Screw the money." Dakota honestly doubted he would get it, and if he did, he feared it would tie him to the cult he wanted to get away from. Plus, Paolo was looking at him with those big brown eyes, and it was making Dakota's libido do a happy dance. "Who wouldn't want you? That's crazy!"

Paolo fluttered his lashes. "Well, there's always the oddball not interested in a sexy man like me." His grin went right to Dakota's balls, making them draw up.

It also did funny things to his heart, but he wasn't going to examine that or give credit to it. He could *not* be falling for a guy he didn't even know. It was just the lust speaking.

"I have a friend who'll let you stay with him," Paolo said. "And you can get your ID, apply for a new one, I think... Well, whatever you need to get, so you can leave, if that's what you want."

"Are you —?" Dakota's heart was pounding. "Are you serious? You'd help me that much?" He bit back the question he wanted to ask along with those, which was why couldn't he stay with Paolo?

"Hasn't anyone ever helped you before?" Paolo asked with such seriousness that Dakota couldn't lie.

"Not really," Dakota answered. "I mean, Utah took me in, but he made sure I knew he'd toss me out if I didn't do what he said at first, then he used the threat of death. That came after I snuck out that time. Then he kind of lost his temper and went on a rant about the Dark Slayers and how he'd committed me to them because I'd agreed and I did but I didn't know they were *really* crazy! And Mom was—"

God, he hated talking about her. Dakota had so many mixed emotions when it came to his mother. "She was hardly ever sober after my father left. I couldn't count on her for much." He should be strong enough not to need anyone's help, yet there he was, letting himself get forced into a screwy cult. "With Utah, I wanted to fit in at first. Bad enough that I went with him willingly to some of the Slayers' meetings, and I even told him I thought it was cool. I thought it was a joke, honestly, but…but it wasn't. Isn't. These people really believe in vampires, and that they should kill them. What if…?" Dakota hated to think about what happened when the Slayers were convinced someone was a vampire. "I'm afraid they've done things. Bad things."

"Then come with me." Paolo slid out of the booth, still holding his hand. "Let me help you."

"Utah said they'd find me, no matter where I ran, if I tried to escape." Dakota scooted along the booth seat until he could stand up. "There's this creepy old guy in the group, Ken, and he's supposed to be some kind of voodoo guy with the power to find me anywhere since he has some of my blood."

"What?" Paolo finally sounded shocked. "How did he get your blood?"

Dakota held up his other hand. There was a healing wound on the tip of one finger. "He cut me, the bastard. I almost passed out when I saw the blood. Thought he was just going to read my palm, not stab my fingertip."

"He took your blood?" Paolo was trying not to shiver. In his culture, way back before he'd been turned, such a thing was akin to having part of one's soul stolen. The medicine men and women from his people would have been able to do many, *many* bad things with Dakota's blood, including

41

making him into their blood slave.

"He did," Dakota confirmed. "He squeezed out blood onto this clamshell like thing then barked at me to get out of his sight. It was weird as hell. Utah said the guy was a new member of that chapter of the Slayers. Apparently there's a lot of them. Chapters, I mean."

Paolo had heard enough for now. It was time to trust his instincts, which were telling him Dakota wasn't scum. *But he might be if he goes through with the initiation. If he doesn't get away. If they brainwash him. Lots of ifs, there.*

He tugged, and Dakota followed him. Utah and Kellan were watching them, as were a couple of other Slayers, Paolo noted. He had no choice but to be in their line of sight if he was going to slip out of the back door with Dakota.

It reminded Paolo of the last time he'd been there, when he and Radney had had a run-in with the Slayers. Radney had saved Paolo, and had suffered some horrible burns from holy water for all his trouble. Claude had healed Radney, but still. It'd been bad.

And they'd escaped out of the back way then, too.

Paolo didn't feel any better about that. "Okay. Act like you can't wait to get my ass on your dick."

Dakota made a strangling sound.

Paolo checked and saw that he was just embarrassed and not actually choking to death on his own tongue. He stopped, then turned and pressed himself against Dakota's lean frame. Paolo slipped a hand to the back of Dakota's nape and used that hold to encourage him to bend his head down.

"Like you were eyeing me up outside, sugar. Don't look scared, look horny, otherwise, they won't think we're going to the back to fuck." Paolo kissed him then, pressing his mouth to Dakota's and pushing his tongue right past Dakota's parted lips when Dakota gasped.

Dakota only hesitated for a second, then he wound his arms around Paolo and moaned as he kissed Paolo back.

Dakota was definitely hard. Paolo felt his dick through

the layers of their clothes—well, mostly Dakota's clothes. Paolo wasn't wearing much, and Dakota was taller, so his cock was pressed right above the waistband of Paolo's shorts, where the mesh shirt had risen up to bare some of Paolo's skin.

Paolo dueled tongues with Dakota, thrusting, swirling, seeking to lay claim just as Dakota was trying to do. It was a dance of power and control, with both of them wanting it, yet both of them giving it over.

When Dakota's hands brushed over Paolo's butt, Paolo's cock leaked pre-cum. His entire body was hot with need, and he didn't question his decision anymore. He simply took a half-step back, ending the kiss, then turned and began tugging on Dakota's hand again.

Paolo kept alert, watching for more Slayers. When he pushed back the curtains to the backroom, a chill went through him. He remembered all too clearly how he'd almost let a Slayer fuck him, had almost ended up dead—

"Hurry," Paolo muttered, more to himself than to Dakota.

"Dak? Where you going? What're you doing?"

Dakota stopped walking. "Utah, I think that's pretty obvious."

Paolo plastered on a smile and turned to face Utah...and Kellan. Paolo wanted to get closer to Kellan—there was something that didn't quite fit with him and the Slayers, but Paolo couldn't pinpoint what it was. Behind Kellan and Utah, Jude slipped into the room. He gave a slight nod, though he didn't look directly at Paolo.

"Yeah, but the others are here, so, you know"—Utah snapped his fingers and leered—"make it quick."

"Uh." Dakota was blushing again. "S-sure."

Paolo stepped in front of Dakota. "Do you think it'll take long for either of us? He gets to fuck this"—Paolo popped himself on the butt—"and I get to have that big dick of his in my ass. I can't wait." He began to pull down his shorts.

"Hey," Jude said, making Utah and Kellan jump. Jude and Kellan locked gazes and an almost electrical current spread through the air before Jude growled and stepped around the Slayers. He looked at Paolo and Dakota. "Can I join in?"

"Yeahokayhurry," Utah babbled even as he spun around and bolted for the safety of the club.

Kellan hesitated a moment, his gaze locked on Jude, who didn't turn around. Another few seconds passed, then Kellan left.

"No, you cannot join in," Paolo informed Jude. "We're trying to split."

Jude sighed and rolled his eyes. "Fine. Guess you two needed rescuing from those idiots, and do I get anything out of being the hero? Nope. I'll just fly out of here. Is there a way out?"

Paolo got the hint. Jude was trusting him and intended to shift into his batty form and follow them.

"Unless you've changed your minds?" Jude prodded. "Haven't heard a word from Slim, here."

Paolo wasn't sure if Jude was teasing or not. He felt the dare in that look, but suspected Jude was just trying to see if Paolo was as cool with Dakota as he seemed. Paolo turned his attention to Dakota, who was frowning at Jude. "Sugar, whatever you want to do."

Dakota tugged Paolo close, but he was looking at Jude. "Are you going to beat me up if I tell you no, we still aren't interested?"

Something that might have been admiration flashed across Jude's features. "Nah, man. Go on. I'm just gonna make sure you two aren't followed. Those guys were talking crazy back there."

Dakota stiffened. "You aren't going to attack us outside?"

Jude laughed, but it sounded forced to Paolo. "Everyone thinks I'm a thug. Go on. Get out of here before they come peeking on you."

Paolo grabbed Dakota's hand and headed for the exit.

Chapter Six

Rather than lead them out of the alley the easy way, toward the street Dakota had walked up with Utah and Kellan, Paolo took a series of turns between buildings and even had them climbing a couple of fences. The big scary guy who wanted to have a threesome didn't follow them.

Dakota wondered if he'd traded one unhinged person for another. He didn't know Paolo at all, and yet he'd pretty much placed his life in the man's hands.

Geez, he really *was* stupid. Dakota just wanted to be able to believe in someone, to trust someone—but maybe he'd have been better off trying to believe in himself for once. He felt like he'd been lost ever since his mom had started drinking heavily, and when she'd died a couple of years ago, his world had spun off its axis and he'd ended up with James.

His mind raced along with his feet. He should have been concentrating on keeping up with Paolo—who was fast as fuck—instead of trying to practice a little introspection.

Paolo didn't let him lag behind, though. He reached back and grabbed Dakota's hand like he'd done at first.

"Almost there," Paolo said, and the man wasn't even breathing hard. Or sweating, Dakota couldn't help but notice.

"Where's there?" Dakota panted out. He was young and in decent shape, but he didn't exercise regularly. The running was wearing him out.

"Mm, a friend's house, like I said," Paolo informed him. "It's just around the corner."

"You aren't even winded," Dakota managed to get out.

Paolo's smile seemed bigger and more genuine than any Dakota had seen from him yet. "Because running was what I did—do. I love it, and it gave me this ass."

There was something odd about that statement, though Dakota couldn't figure out just what.

"One more turn," Paolo promised. Once they'd made it, they stopped running.

Dakota looked around, kind of dizzy and light-headed from the exercise. They must have run for at least an hour.

"Thirty minutes," Paolo said.

Dakota hadn't realized he'd spoken out loud. "Nuh uh." He looked around the neighborhood where they'd stopped. "Where are we?"

"Somewhere safe, almost." Paolo adjusted the waistband of his shorts, then winced and reached behind him. "Damn. These are *not* made to run in. Talk about the wedgie from hell. Eesh. And my feet are going to fall off. Running in heels—women make it look easy, but it *so* isn't."

That made Dakota laugh. "I could help you with the wedgie," he surprised himself by saying. Flirting wasn't something he was used to doing.

Paolo winked at him. "Oh, sugar, you'll be playing with my ass soon, unless you want me to fuck you instead. I could *so* do that."

Dakota clenched his butt. He'd had anal sex before, with James, who'd always topped. He really wanted to know what that was like. "Could I, um, do you?"

"Do me?" Paolo shook his head. "Sugar, if you can't say it, you shouldn't do it." He fisted one hand on a cocked hip and waited.

Dakota felt himself blushing. "C-could I f-fuck you?" Wow, he'd only stuttered twice. "I never have. Topped, I mean." His own admission made him panic. "Oh, so you should probably fuck me, or we could suck each other off, or—"

"No, sugar," Paolo said, his voice dropping deeper as he reached out and cupped Dakota's cock through his jeans.

"I want this monster in my ass. You've got a good dick on you."

"James said it was too big." Dakota really wished he could keep such embarrassing admissions to himself.

"Too big?" Paolo rubbed Dakota's shaft. "No such thing. Your ex was a fool."

Dakota wanted to say something intelligent, but the feel of Paolo's hand was making him forget how to speak. He did whimper, which would have been embarrassing, had Dakota the fortitude to care. As it was, all the blood in his body had rushed to his dick, so he couldn't even blush.

"I want all of it," Paolo said. "Wish I could let you fuck me without a condom. I mean, you *can* —"

"I'm not on the meds to prevent HIV," Dakota said. "I don't have that kind of money."

Paolo nodded. "Yeah, I've heard of it. I don't have anything you can catch, but I don't expect you to take my word for it. I know Erin will have a few condoms. Hopefully they will be big enough to fit you."

"A few condoms?" Dakota tried to keep the hope out of his voice.

"Just for tonight. We'll need a lot more for tomorrow and so on," Paolo explained. "I mean, if you want to hook up again after tonight."

Dakota couldn't imagine himself getting tired of Paolo anytime soon, and maybe not ever. Then he silently scolded himself, because he really shouldn't be thinking like that. Like they had a future.

But he became aware of something — Paolo was waiting for him to speak. Dakota thought about Paolo's last words. "I can't imagine not wanting you."

Paolo's wide smile was back. "Well, good. You can have me tonight. Then we'll discuss options." The smile died down. "I didn't think you wanted to stay in Vegas, so we'll have to figure out where you do want to go, and how to help you get there."

"Why are you helping me?" Dakota asked, even as he

thrust his hips, seeking more of Paolo's touch.

"Because it would be wrong of me to leave you in the hands of crazy cultists," Paolo said. "Plus, I like you, or what I know of you so far."

That was good enough for Dakota. "And this Erin, who is she?"

"He. Erin is my best friend's ma—er, husband's twin brother," Paolo explained. "He's probably out screwing some twink, but I know where he keeps his spare key."

Dakota wanted to ask if Erin would be cool with them raiding his condoms but thought better of it. He was just going to trust Paolo's judgment. He had excellent judgment, knowing just how hard to stroke Dakota's cock, how fast— and when to step away, which Paolo did then.

"Don't want you to come yet," Paolo said. "Though you're young—you'd probably get hard again in ten minutes."

"I'm twenty-four. How old are you?" Dakota asked, promptly taking Paolo's hand when it was offered. He liked Paolo's skin, which was cooler than his, and soft, so soft. Considering the arid climate, that was a miracle in itself. Dakota stroked the back of Paolo's hand.

Paolo purred. *Purred!* Which maybe should have been weird, but Dakota liked it. It scattered Dakota's thoughts, and the kiss Paolo followed it up with made Dakota forget what they'd been discussing.

"Come on. I want you," Paolo murmured against Dakota's lips.

Dakota might have said *Me too*, or he might have just squeaked. It was hard to tell which with his pulse pounding in his ears. He followed almost mindlessly as Paolo led him to a house with a small porch.

Dakota noticed the rose bushes edging the railing, which brought him back to himself. He had always loved roses, but killed every plant he'd had. He wondered what colors the blooms would be when they opened. With the streetlamp and the porch light, it was impossible for him to tell.

The house itself was older, but seemed well-maintained.

The siding was white and the windows were trimmed in dark shutters. Something flapped past Dakota, just out of sight.

Dakota shivered and moved closer to Paolo. He looked at the darkness again, thought he heard some flapping, and turned his gaze to Paolo and the front of the house.

The door was a bright red, and Paolo was opening it. Dakota had missed him retrieving the key, not that it mattered.

"Yeah, Erin's not here," Paolo said as he gestured at Dakota to go in. "He'd have been standing here giving me shit if he was."

Dakota stepped inside and glanced around. He saw pictures on the wall closest to him, parents and two boys who had to be twins.

"That's Erin and Andrew," Paolo said. "Their parents passed away years ago. Erin kept the house. Andrew lives with Radney. And that's enough talking, unless it's dirty talk. Come fuck me, sugar. Show me that big dick of yours."

Dakota gave a fleeting thought to Utah, and what he might be doing, whether or not he was worried or pissed off that Dakota had disappeared. Then Paolo stepped back, and without hesitation, turned around and pulled his shorts down, baring his ass to Dakota.

Dakota moved as if in a trance. He had to touch that smooth, honey-brown skin and see if it was as soft as it looked.

Paolo shimmied, maybe moving his shorts down to his ankles, maybe shivering, Dakota didn't know which. He sighed as he placed his hands on Paolo's plump cheeks.

"Oh...man, you feel so good," Dakota murmured, giving the flesh under his palms a squeeze.

"Your touch feels good to me, too, sugar," Paolo said as he pushed his bottom back. "Let's get to a bed, and you can grope me all you want."

Dakota traced the seam of Paolo's ass with one finger, then reluctantly stopped touching him as Paolo straightened up.

"This way," Paolo said, pulling his mesh shirt off and tossing it behind him as he strode down a hall.

Dakota caught the shirt, and scooped up Paolo's shorts for good measure. He didn't know Erin, but thought the guy probably wouldn't like coming home to a trail of clothes. Or two pieces of clothing.

And Paolo still had on his ankle boots. For some reason, that sparked Dakota's lust higher. He trotted after Paolo, watching the way the heels of those boots struck the wood floor.

Then he raised his gaze up and watched Paolo's butt flex and bounce as he walked. Paolo had very little body hair, Dakota noted. Even his crack hadn't been very fuzzy, not like James'. Dakota would have sworn a person could stash a small fortune in jewels in James' hairy ass crack and never find it again. Rimming him had been an adventure in flossing.

"Mind on me, sugar," Paolo ordered, peering over his shoulder at Dakota.

Dakota blinked and shook his head. "How'd you know—?"

"You were frowning fit to be tied, and I *know* this sweet ass wasn't making you miserable." Paolo turned around and patted his right cheek. "Now stop thinking about that ex and concentrate on me."

"How'd you know—?" Dakota began again, only to be cut off.

"Because only an ex would put that look of misery on a man's face." Paolo smiled again, that wide, happy, welcoming smile that made Dakota feel tingly inside.

Paolo just seemed so glad to be there with him. In fact, not once during their admittedly short acquaintance had Paolo done or said anything to make Dakota feel like a dork or a loser.

Dakota could fall for him, so easily.

"It's been a long time since anyone's fucked me," Paolo was saying, backing into a room. He flipped on a light switch. "Well, since I've had sex, period."

"How long?" Dakota asked. Surely a man as sexy as Paolo didn't go for more than a few days without sex, unless he just didn't want to do it.

"A few years," Paolo informed him.

Dakota stopped just inside the room and gawked at him. "That's — that's longer than it's been for me!"

Paolo shrugged elegantly. "What can I say? I'm picky, and maybe I was waiting for you."

Though he said it in a teasing way, his voice light and lyrical, Dakota wished Paolo meant it. Wondered if maybe he had.

And there Dakota went again, being weird and needy, reading someone wrong again. Paolo was out to get laid, nothing more, and for some odd reason, he'd decided it was Dakota he wanted to have sex with. *But he said he'd help me too. He's going to help me get away from Utah and the Slayers. Why is he doing that? Who does things like that now days?*

Paolo sighed loudly. "I can see I'm going to have to help you keep focused. I do love a challenge."

Dakota started to stutter out an apology, but Paolo slid to his knees right *there* in front of him, and Paolo's hands were on Dakota's waistband, then Paolo was popping open the button, unzipping Dakota's jeans —

"Sweet, sugar," Paolo said right before he shoved Dakota's jeans and briefs down in one quick move. "So pretty. I love a veiny dick."

"Thanks?" Dakota wasn't certain what manners applied to penis compliments, but he figured 'thanks' ought to be okay.

Paolo gazed up at him. For the first time, Dakota had a good look at his eyes in decent lighting. They were very dark brown, almost as dark as his pupils, but the irises were ringed on the outside in a milky gray color. Paolo had short lashes, but they were very thick, so dense in fact that at first, Dakota thought Paolo had eyeliner on his bottom lids.

Paolo winked at him, and lightly gripped Dakota's cock.

"Touch me. Put your hands on me."

Dakota's hands shook as he raised them, holding them right above Paolo's shoulders. "Are you sure?" James hadn't liked for Dakota to hold on to him when James gave him head.

Paolo sighed. "Oh, sugar, someone's been an asshole to you. Yes, I'm sure. I want you to let go and just fuck my mouth."

Dakota almost came on the spot. He had a little trouble breathing, he was so excited, as he dared to place one hand on Paolo's left shoulder, and his other along Paolo's jaw.

"Perfect," Paolo said. He lowered his gaze, leaned forward, and licked over Dakota's slit. "Mmm, yummy." He licked again, then a third time.

Dakota remembered to inhale, though it seemed hard to do, like the air itself was thick with lust. His breath shot out of him when Paolo sucked on the crown of his cock, taking the head into his hot, wet mouth. He did something with his tongue, flicking, moving it, and Dakota clenched his hands, trying to hold himself back.

Paolo made a rumbling noise, and it caused some amazing vibrations against Dakota's shaft. He forgot to restrain himself as he gave in to the need to thrust. His cock went deep, with Paolo taking it and taking it in, until the head slipped into his throat.

Dakota tried to say how good it felt, but the "Arngh!" he got out might not have got his message across.

Or perhaps it had, since Paolo rumbled again, and he turned those dark eyes up to look at Dakota.

And smiled, his lips quirking right before he swallowed.

"Oh fuck!" Dakota yelped, then he lost it, pulling back, thrusting in, so hard and fast, it was all a blur. He thought he'd only just started to move when his balls tightened and cum shot up to his dick. His brain screamed at him to warn Paolo. "Coming—"

Paolo sucked harder, and Dakota's head spun as he came, feeling his orgasm in every cell of his being. It was more intense than anything he'd ever experienced with James, or by himself.

Dakota whimpered as he chased that fleeting pleasure, wishing he could stay lost in ecstasy forever. He couldn't, and he came back to himself in little, hyper-sensitive increments.

Paolo seemed to know when Dakota was about to overload and pulled off, letting Dakota's penis slip from his mouth.

"Sweet," Paolo pronounced, and his voice was rough, nothing like the smooth tones of earlier.

Dakota had done that to him, ramming his cock into Paolo's mouth, fucking his throat without concern. "Shit," Dakota muttered, dropping to his knees. "I'm so sorry! I—"

Paolo startled him by pinching his butt. "None of that. Best blow job I've gotten to give in possibly ever, sugar."

"But... But... I didn't take care of you." Dakota struggled to explain his worries. He had been totally selfish, and not even aware of whether or not he might have been hurting Paolo.

Paolo startled him with a loud, joyous laugh. "Oh, you sweet man, don't you know that you gave me just what I wanted? I wanted your control, sugar, wanted you stripped bare for me."

Then Paolo smiled and for one weird second, Dakota thought he saw the sharp tips of a couple of teeth— noticeably sharper than people's teeth normally were. He dismissed it as his imagination running awry due to lack of proper blood flow to his brain.

Paolo took Dakota's hands in his, then guided them down to Paolo's erection. "I drove you wild. Now, you're going to do the same for me."

Chapter Seven

Paolo moaned when Dakota began stroking him. He could have kept quiet, but something told him Dakota needed all the encouragement and confidence boosting he could get. Paolo wasn't giving him a pity fuck, though. No, he wasn't. Dakota was sexy and sweet and innocent — *well, almost innocent* — and he really *did* have a huge dick that Paolo wanted to feel spreading his ass open.

Plus, Paolo was preventing the birth or creation of another Dark Slayer. Claude might not approve of his methods, but Paolo could deal with Claude's displeasure. He couldn't deal with walking away from Dakota and leaving him in the hands of murderers, or would-be murderers. Either one was bad.

And having Dakota jack him off was awesome. It also wasn't enough.

"Fuck me," Paolo demanded, clutching at Dakota. "Bend me over and fuck me until I scream."

"Oh Jesus," Dakota whimpered. "Condoms, I need the condoms!"

Paolo almost told him that no, he most certainly *didn't* need condoms. Vampires really didn't have to worry about STDs. But then he'd have to explain that he *was* a vampire, and that conversation would go south quickly.

"I'll get 'em," Paolo offered. "Get on the bed. I'll be right back."

"'Kay." Dakota gave him one more stroke, then he let go of Paolo's cock. "Lube —"

"I'll get it." Paolo sprang to his feet, surprised to feel kind of shaky in the legs. No one had aroused him as much as

Dakota did. It was strange, and he wanted to explore it with Dakota. One night wouldn't be enough for that.

He'd just have to come visit Dakota at Erin's, that was all there was to it.

Paolo rushed to the guest bathroom and found the condoms and lube right where he'd hoped they'd be. Erin had become a friend of his, although they weren't best buddies or anything. Still, they were close enough that Paolo knew some things about Erin and was welcome in his house, an important thing for a vampire when it came to entering a home.

And he knew where the condoms and lube were.

He took them back to the bedroom, then paused a few feet away from the bed, just to admire the view.

Dakota blushed, the pink from his cheeks spreading all the way down to his chest. "What?" he asked, moving his hands down as if to cover his erection.

"Don't," Paolo said. "If you hide that pretty cock from me, I'll cry."

"Can't have that," Dakota replied, a slight smile appearing as he moved his hands to his sides.

"Nope." Paolo held up the supplies. "You want to get me ready? If not, that's okay. I can prep my own ass, no problem."

"I want—" Dakota swallowed, his throat clicking. "I want everything you'll give me. I want to try it all, if you'll let me. If you'd like it."

Paolo wanted to throttle the man who had made Dakota feel like he didn't deserve to enjoy sex. He buried his anger and closed the distance between him and Dakota. "Everything and all of it might take a while. Longer than one night."

Paolo was prepared to act silly and flirty if Dakota didn't take the hint, or outright rejected the idea of them spending more than one night together.

Dakota sat up and held his hands out for the condoms and lube. "Okay, if... If you're willing."

"Of course I'm willing," Paolo responded, almost giggling in relief. He settled for bouncing onto the bed instead. "I think we'll have fun together."

Dakota nodded. "I hope so. I... I'm usually not this impulsive. It took me six weeks of dating James to have sex with him. I mean, it was hand jobs, but still. Caution didn't do me any good, so I'm going to listen to my instincts from now on. They told me to run when I first met Utah, and I ignored them. But tonight—" He smiled broadly, his pretty eyes gleaming with happiness. "Tonight, I felt like I should talk to you, and follow you. And... And fuck you," he added in a quieter voice.

"Definitely that last one," Paolo agreed. He grinned and turned around, settling onto his hands and knees with his ass presented to Dakota. The gasp from Dakota plumped up Paolo's ego, and his dick grew even harder than it'd been. "So get me ready, sugar. A cock as big as yours is going to require some prep."

Dakota inhaled, exhaled then huffed. "This is really embarrassing, but I'd rather be embarrassed than hurt you. I haven't ever topped."

Paolo felt something warm and affectionate budding inside him at the admission. "I'll tell you if you hurt me, I promise. Just use lots of lube and enjoy prepping me."

"I will." Dakota surprised him then by scooting closer and kissing his left butt cheek. "Can I...?"

"Whatever you want," Paolo rasped, trying not to get his hopes up. He couldn't recall the last time he'd been rimmed.

"This," Dakota murmured, his breath fanning across Paolo's skin. "I want this." He spread Paolo's cheeks. "I want in here."

Paolo's eyes rolled back at the first hesitant touch of Dakota's tongue over his hole. He lowered himself until his shoulders were on the bed, his head turned, mouth open on a moan.

Dakota's first few licks were light, as if he was learning as he went. Paolo didn't mind if that was the case. He liked

Dakota more than he could remember liking anyone so quickly.

Another lick, then Dakota pressed in closer, nosing the skin above Paolo's pucker while lapping harder at that delicate spot. He let go of Paolo's cheeks and started caressing his back and butt, his thighs and belly. Dakota skirted around Paolo's cock, not quite touching it, and that was driving Paolo crazy, pushing his lust up to new levels.

Then Dakota settled his hands over Paolo's hip bones, and pulled him back as Dakota pressed his tongue past Paolo's ring.

"Da—" Paolo gulped, flushing hot with arousal. "Dakota!" His voice broke and he opened his eyes just enough to register light. He moaned and arched his lower back as Dakota rimmed him, pushing, pulling, controlling Paolo's hips.

Paolo gave himself over to Dakota, let him lead. It wasn't often that Paolo willingly gave any man power over him when it came to sex, but he wanted Dakota to be in control.

Dakota moaned as he licked into Paolo, and he kept squeezing Paolo's hips, as if he were afraid Paolo would jolt and disappear.

It wouldn't happen. Paolo was Dakota's to use as he wanted.

A slick finger joined Dakota's tongue. It felt good, then it felt even better as Dakota sat up and pushed more fingers in him, two, then three, until Paolo was mewling, scrambling to hold on to the covers every time Dakota massaged his prostate.

"Now," Dakota said in a stripped voice. "I have to fuck you now."

"Yes," Paolo hissed. To his surprise, his fangs dropped down and he narrowly missed spearing his own tongue. He clamped his mouth shut and buried his face in the pillow, ashamed of himself for losing control.

At least Dakota hadn't spotted his fangs. That would have been a mood-killer.

Paolo heard Dakota opening the condom package, then he listened to the sound of Dakota's shaky breaths and the squelch of lube after Dakota sheathed his cock with the protection.

The bed dipped as Dakota moved, and Paolo nearly begged him to please hurry up.

Dakota was behind him. He lined his dick up, the covered tip against Paolo's hole, and clamped one hand on Paolo's hip.

"Oh, fuck," Dakota drawled as he began to press against Paolo's furled opening.

Paolo willed his muscles to relax, and he pushed out at just the right moment.

"Augh!" Dakota yelped, spreading Paolo's ring wide with the crown of his cock. "So...tight. Hot. Hot and soft and—" He thrust, then did it again, harder.

Paolo couldn't believe the sounds he was making, the needy, hungry noises that slipped past his lips as Dakota worked his cock into him. Everything about this, about sex with Dakota, felt different from anything Paolo had shared with anyone else.

He couldn't focus on trying to figure out why that was, not when Dakota's hips were finally pressed up against Paolo's ass.

"Paolo, I can't— I need to move," Dakota rasped, his hand tightening on Paolo.

"Please," Paolo begged, clenching and flexing his butt. "Fuck me hard."

"Yeah." Dakota pulled almost all the way out, then thrust back in. "I will. So hard."

And he did, hammering into Paolo like a man desperate to fuck, craving release. Paolo tried to slam back and meet him thrust for thrust, but Dakota covered him, pressing his chest to Paolo's back, holding on to him, *holding* him.

Paolo couldn't do anything but take the rough fucking. He gave himself over to it, to Dakota's care, without question.

His ass stung around the rim, his inner walls grew hotter

with friction. Need coiled tighter and tighter in his gut, and Paolo was pushed closer to the edge.

Before he could reach it, Dakota sat up, his cock still inside Paolo. "On your back. I want to see your face when you come." He pulled out completely and reached for the lube as Paolo shakily moved to lie on his back.

He was shivering, maybe only internally, and his fangs were still an issue. Paolo tried to will them away as he kept his lips pressed together.

"What's wrong?" Dakota asked, hand hovering above his shaft, both glistening with lubrication. His eyebrows were nearly touching above his nose as he studied Paolo.

Paolo was scared enough of being found out as a vampire that he managed to get his fangs under control. "Nothing. Just need you back in me."

Dakota studied him a second longer then, his expression still intense, Dakota moved between Paolo's legs.

Once Dakota finished slicking up his cock, he lined it up.

Paolo held his legs up, knees to chest, but Dakota shook his head.

"I want your legs around me."

Paolo had no desire to argue. He spread his legs as Dakota thrust slowly, filling Paolo with no rush at all, even though Paolo could smell Dakota's need.

Dakota lowered himself over Paolo again, and he kissed Paolo before he began to fuck him. Kissed Paolo even as they moved together, Paolo curling his ass up as much as he could when Dakota thrust into him.

Paolo's climax was building again, a slow, heavy roll of pleasure coming up from his ass to his balls, spreading throughout his body when Dakota reached between them and fisted Paolo's dick.

He didn't last long then. Paolo arched and cried out as he came, as his senses swelled and ecstasy overloaded every nerve in his body. He heard his name called out, felt Dakota stiffen in him, above him, the tight grip of Dakota's hand going slack.

Paolo couldn't seem to get his breath back, not in a timely manner. He had, at some point, closed his eyes, and he opened them to discover that Dakota had collapsed on top of him.

There were still tendrils of bliss rippling through him, gentling him down to reality. Paolo buried one hand in Dakota's hair and tried again to get a good breath.

Dakota mumbled something and slid to Paolo's side.

Paolo wanted to stay there with Dakota, sleep with him until morning, but he couldn't. He needed to check in with Jude and Claude, and let Erin know what was up—and he'd have to get to the safe room Erin had set up for vamps. Paolo could have taken Dakota there, but had feared the questions Dakota might ask if he realized the curtains in the room were hung over bare wall, not actual windows.

Before Paolo could decide how to do everything that needed doing, and not vanish on Dakota, he heard the bedroom door open, just a slight hiss of a sound.

Paolo turned his head and saw Erin, then Jude with him, peering in.

Paolo sighed quietly, and slid out of the bed without waking Dakota. He had much to do, and lying there, wishing he could stay by Dakota, wasn't going to keep him safe.

Chapter Eight

It was the voices that woke him up. Dakota was confused at first, waking in a strange bed, a strange room…and alone. The last one irked him because he definitely remembered Paolo being there with him, remembered the way Paolo's eyes had gone wide as he'd moaned, his lips parting and —

He sat up so fast it made him dizzy. His heart was racing and he rubbed at his chest as he replayed the moment Paolo had climaxed, the tight squeeze of his ass around Dakota's cock, the slick spread of cum over Dakota's hand, the expression on Paolo's face.

His mind zoomed in on that image, specifically on Paolo's mouth.

"No, no, no," Dakota muttered, pressing harder on his chest. He closed his eyes and saw it again, Paolo, so perfect and gorgeous as he came apart under Dakota, mouth dropping open. *Fangs.*

"No," he repeated, shaking his head. "No way did I see fangs!"

Almost immediately, there was a knock on the bedroom door, and Dakota squeaked in surprise. He jerked the blanket up to his armpits, realized there was the barest hint of sunlight peeking around the blinds, and he was in a stranger's house, without Paolo there.

What *was* the proper response to someone knocking on the door when it wasn't Dakota's house? It had to be the owner, Erin. At least, Dakota hoped that was who it was. "Er, come in?" he called out when another series of knocks sounded.

The door opened, and an attractive dark-haired man

entered the room. He wasn't Paolo, however.

"Where's Paolo?" Dakota asked without thinking.

The man grinned crookedly. "Hi, nice to meet you, Dakota. I'm Erin. Welcome to my humble abode."

Dakota felt himself blushing. "Uh, yeah, sorry. I'm—" *Has Paolo told him why I'm here?*

Erin laughed and came right over to the bed then sat on the side of it, one knee cocked toward Dakota on the mattress, foot tucked under Erin's butt. The other foot was on the floor.

Erin was dressed in a dark pair of jeans and a long-sleeved T-shirt. He had nice features, but he didn't turn Dakota's crank.

"So, Dakota. I hear you've escaped from a cult," Erin began, peering so intently at Dakota that it made him squirm.

Dakota's skin prickled with goosebumps despite him being under the covers for the most part. Would Erin think he was crazy? "Some—" And had he *really* seen fangs when Paolo had come? Dakota hoped he sounded calm. "Yeah. What'd Paolo tell you? And where is he? Is he allergic to sunlight?" His heart pounded as he made the joke that wasn't really a joke.

Erin sighed and tilted his head to the left as he touched his chin. "Oh, my. What a strange question to ask, and I know I heard you say something about fangs before I knocked on the door. I have to wonder if the cult hasn't already gotten to you."

"You heard me say what?" Dakota pushed himself up until his back was against the headboard. He let the bedding pool around his hips. "What were you doing, pressing your ear to the door?" Rude or not, he wasn't going to put up with Erin lurking and listening.

Erin snorted. "Right, like you didn't almost screech it. What's your octave range?"

Dakota started to shove the blanket and sheet all the way off, intending to get up and storm out—until he remembered

62

he was nude. He had to settle for glaring at Erin.

"Look, I'm not trying to be a dick," Erin began before smiling again. "That part just comes naturally. You want to know where Paolo went? He's here, sleeping in the other room. He didn't want you to feel pressured for morning sex or anything."

"I'm not buying it," Dakota replied. Something didn't feel right about...everything.

"It's true. I can show you where he is." Erin stood. "If you want to get dressed and follow me. Or come along naked. I don't mind. After you've seen him, you can tell me why you were screeching about fangs."

Dakota intended to do no such thing. He decided that he wasn't staying in Erin's house either. He'd go check on Paolo, and tell him goodbye.

"Oh, stop being so grumpy." Erin strolled to the bedroom door. "I'm just worried about Paolo if that cult got to you."

"Why?" Dakota asked. Was it because Paolo was— No, Dakota couldn't think that. It was crazy.

"Because if you think he's a vampire, which it sounds like you do, then you might be inclined to kill him, or try to," Erin added, "and I happen to like Paolo. He's a good guy."

But is he a vampire? Dakota didn't voice the question. *Vampires don't exist. It's just the weeks of stress with the Dark Slayers. It's got my head screwed up.* "Vampires aren't real." *There. That sounded sane.*

Erin didn't reply. He left the bedroom and pulled the door almost all the way shut behind him.

Dakota rolled out of bed, holding the sheet around him just in case Erin or someone who wasn't Paolo decided to come walking in uninvited. He found his clothes and put them back on, except for his socks and shoes. He couldn't bring himself to put dirty socks back on. And he *really* needed a shower.

There was a bathroom attached to the bedroom. Dakota took care of some basic hygiene and emptied his bladder, then he checked himself in the mirror and figured he didn't look half bad for being him. With a shrug, he turned away and went to find Erin.

Who was waiting right out in the hallway for him.

"That's a little creepy, you know," Dakota grumbled, stopping just outside the bedroom to frown at Erin.

Erin smirked at him. "Why? I knew you were coming out here. Wouldn't want you to have to hunt me—or Paolo—down. Tell me, did you even see the rest of the house last night, or did Paolo keep you too busy?"

Dakota flushed with warmth, thinking about Paolo last night. His dick was going to get hard if he didn't rein in his thoughts, though, so he instead focused on Erin. As cute as the man was, he did nothing for Dakota. "I just want to talk to Paolo."

"If he's awake, sure." Erin nodded then gestured to a door down the hall. "He's right there. Let's peek in on him, shall we?" He closed the door to the room Dakota had just left. "This way."

For some reason, Dakota was incredibly nervous. He was sweating, which was gross, and he was confused as to why he was worried. It wasn't until Erin opened the door to the bedroom where Paolo lay sleeping on a tall bed that Dakota relaxed. As much as he hated to admit it, he'd been afraid Erin would open that door and there'd be a coffin in the room. He was totally screwed up thanks to the Slayers.

The bedroom was very dark. There were curtains, and not even the barest hint of light peeked around them.

"Satisfied?" Erin asked, standing in front of Dakota and partially blocking the doorway.

Dakota stared at Paolo. He seemed very still. It was hard to tell without a light turned on, but he looked like he wasn't breathing. "Is he okay?" Dakota whispered to Erin.

Erin started to back out and close the door. "Sure. He's out like a light."

Dakota slapped a hand against the door to prevent Erin from shutting it. "Hang on just a minute."

"You're going to wake him up," Erin warned, still trying

to close the door.

Dakota couldn't shake the funny feeling he had that something wasn't right, or that Erin was trying to pull the wool over his eyes. He pushed and Erin pulled as they glared at each other.

Paolo didn't seem to be waking up, despite the scuffling.

Dakota grinned at Erin and poked him in the ribs.

Erin screeched, and he let go of the door. As he did, he stumbled and fell into the room.

Dakota stepped over him and rushed to the bed. Dread filled him. He was suddenly terrified. The room was dark, except for light coming in from the hallway. Something wasn't right. Dakota couldn't put his finger on what, but he knew it.

His hands shook as he raised one, intending to touch Paolo's cheek.

"Don't!" Erin grabbed his hand. "He doesn't react well to being startled awake. That's why he sleeps alone."

Dakota didn't look at Erin. "Yeah? I thought he didn't want me to feel pressured for sex. So which is it?"

Erin cursed and Dakota jerked his hand away. He touched Paolo's cheek, a little harder than he'd meant to, but without bad intent.

Paolo's eyes snapped open, and the red glow to them both terrified Dakota and didn't surprise him at the same time. It was like his mind was divided into two halves, one that said *Well duh, 'cause he's a vampire, ya moron*, and the other *Get the fuck out of here! Run!* Dakota was frozen in place.

"Fuck," Erin groaned. "Damn it!" He shoved at Dakota. "Paolo, go back to sleep!"

"No." Dakota shoved Erin back. "Don't." He definitely saw the glint of white fangs when Paolo yawned.

"Aw, hell." Erin sighed and plopped his butt on the bed.

"What?" Paolo asked with a slight lisp as he started to sit up. His eyes went wide. The red in them vanished.

Dakota knew he'd seen it, just like he'd seen fangs. He stumbled away, spinning after a few steps so he could bolt to the door.

But Paolo was faster.

Dakota stared in horror as Paolo shot past him, moving so quickly he was more of a blur than not, and slammed the door shut.

Shit, he'd really gone from being screwed to probably dead in a matter of minutes. Dakota drew back one fisted hand —

Paolo cringed and turned his head aside. "Go ahead."

"Why — ?" Dakota cleared his throat. His arm was already beginning to ache and his fingers were going numb. His heart was beating so fast, he feared that he might have a heart attack.

Paolo still didn't face him.

"Calm down," Erin said from behind Dakota. "He's not going to hurt you." Then he added, "Paolo, I'm going to turn the lamp by the bed on."

There was *click*, then soft light chased away most of the darkness.

Dakota finally lowered his arm, unclenched his fist. He was shaking so hard that his teeth were chattering. *When did* that *happen?*

Paolo took a loud, stuttering breath but didn't speak. He exhaled as if he'd been gut-punched. It made his cock bounce, even though that part of him was soft.

"Dakota," Erin said. "Don't hurt Paolo."

Dakota moved quickly, trying to stand where he could see Erin, who'd been behind him, and Paolo. "Are you...? Are you...?" He couldn't say it out loud.

"No, I'm not a vampire. Just a psychiatrist, and a human." Erin moved a few steps toward Paolo. "I can show you my degrees, if you'd like. For the psychiatry, I mean. Obviously."

Dakota had heard many times that most people went into psychology and psychiatry to figure out what was wrong with themselves. Maybe that wasn't true, but he wasn't discounting it in Erin's case. The man was entirely too calm.

Paolo hadn't moved—he held himself still like some kind of living doorstop.

"I can't talk about any of this"—Erin waved a hand at Paolo—"but I can get you someone who *is* allowed to discuss it. My brother, Andrew."

"I don't want to talk to your brother," Dakota snapped. "I'd ask if you're crazy but I think we both know the answer to that."

Erin grinned at him. "Good, I'm glad you understand how very sane and reasonable I am."

Dakota wanted to deck him, especially when he moved closer to Paolo again.

"Paolo," Erin said quietly. "Are you okay?"

Paolo gave the barest of nods.

Erin shot Dakota a dirty look that clearly said, *this is your fault, asshole!*

Dakota shouldn't have felt guilty, yet he did.

"Good," Erin continued, turning his attention back to Paolo. "I have to say, you look a little tense, buddy. Is there something you need?"

Paolo licked his lips.

Dakota's heart just about beat right out of his chest.

"N-no," Paolo said a moment later. "I took care of it last night."

Every word he spoke sounded off.

Dakota supposed it was the fangs. Paolo still had them.

"So you're calm?" Erin asked, almost reaching Paolo.

"I'm not Radney," Paolo grumbled. "Not that he's bad anymore."

"Oh, that's—" Erin spun and Dakota didn't know what happened. There was pain in his head, then…there was nothing but darkness.

Chapter Nine

"You didn't have to hit him!" Paolo exclaimed. At least he'd caught Dakota before he hit the floor. "What if you seriously hurt him?"

"I didn't," Erin replied. "I have my black belt in—"

"I don't care what you have it in," Paolo snapped. He began to carry Dakota to the bed. "I didn't want him hurt."

"He would have hit you if he hadn't thought you'd kill him." Erin shrugged. "Plus, it was a chance to see if that pinch would really work. He's really skinny. Heroin chic, or naturally thin?"

"Erin," Paolo growled, exasperated by the man. "Can you stop being an ass?"

"Probably not. And on that note, I'm going to go call Andrew, and Claude, I guess. Can't have him thinking I narc'd about vampires. I prefer to keep my memories." Erin left the room.

"At least he's honest about being an ass," Paolo murmured as he laid Dakota out on the bed. "I don't even know where he hit you. Pinched you. Whatever he did. I'm so sorry, sugar."

Dakota groaned and squirmed, then his eyes snapped open and he gasped. "Don't bite me!"

Paolo's fangs had been giving him trouble, mainly because he liked Dakota, and yes, he wanted to feed from him. Paolo had tried to deny that urge, but it wouldn't go away. He'd never force himself on anyone, though. The very idea did what he'd been trying to do and sent his fangs away. "I wouldn't, ever." It occurred to him that he should have denied that he was a vampire in the first place. If he'd tried hard enough, he might have convinced Dakota that the whole episode had been a dream.

Except he didn't want to lie to Dakota. The poor guy had been manipulated enough. Chances were good, however, that Claude would show up after sunset and erase all the memories Dakota had of vampires existing. Paolo doubted he'd be able to talk Claude out of doing that. Maybe he could ask Claude to erase the memories of Utah—

No. No way will I help dabble with his brain. "We aren't monsters," Paolo blurted, lowering himself to sit on the floor beside the bed. "We *aren't*." The rug was scratchy under his legs and butt. He wished he could sit on the bed or cuddle on it with Dakota. "I mean, some vampires are, just like some humans are monsters. It's… It's not what we are, but who we are inside that makes us good or bad."

Dakota's eyes had gotten wider with every sentence Paolo spoke. "R-right. S-sure."

Paolo shrank down, pulling his knees to his chest and hunching over, trying to look small and not dangerous. "It's true. My coven, we are all decent people. We aren't dead. We're alive, and we have feelings and dreams, regrets and needs."

"L-like blood," Dakota said in an accusatory tone.

There was no use denying that one. "Yes, like blood, but we don't attack anyone for it. There are a lot of people who are into vampire play, who beg to be bitten." He raised his head and looked at Dakota again. "No killing. It doesn't take a lot of blood to keep us going. There's also bagged blood, and probably some animals we could live on, but *those* would have to be killed. Besides, most of the times with humans, our bites are highly erotic. It's not unusual for someone to come from getting bitten."

Dakota just stared at him and Paolo felt inclined to continue talking.

"All we want to do is live. What we have to do in order for that to be possible—drink blood-- we have no choice in that. People have blood transfusions to survive. No one thinks they're monsters. When…" Paolo closed his eyes, letting his mind drift back. "When I was turned, I was twenty. It was long ago, and I was a hunter. My people believed in gods and goddesses, signs and portents. When *he* floated down from the sky and stood before me, I thought he was a god. I walked right into his embrace, and what I said about bites?" He swallowed back the memory of the terror that had hit him so long ago. "That's true in most cases now, but then, with *him*, there was nothing good about it. He took great pleasure in hurting me, in scaring me, telling me how he was going to rip into me and make me scream with pain."

Paolo held himself tighter. "And he did, then he left me there to die, left me for the sun to claim. I would have been ash if Corlo, my brother, hadn't seen what happened. He waited until my sire left, then dragged me into the darkest cave. Corlo saved me, and he never turned me away. When he died, I went mad. Claude found me. I don't know how, or why, but he did. I know Claude killed my original sire, but I claim Claude as my maker."

"You can just…change that?"

Upon hearing Dakota's question, Paolo almost smiled.

"I was mad, both kinds of mad when Claude found me. I was also starving, because Corlo, my brother, had also supplied me with blood. Usually his, but occasionally, not." Paolo shrugged. "I never asked him where he got it. A vampire without blood is a dangerous thing. I didn't harm anyone. I wouldn't, not then, not now. Claude found me, fed me, and made me one of his coven members. I trust him like no other. I have never killed anyone." He bit back the *sugar*. He didn't think he deserved to get to use the endearment now. "Not even when I was crazy from lack of blood. It's not in me to kill, or I'd have gone and decimated the enemy tribe that ended my brother's life."

"You couldn't turn him into…into…"

Paolo waited, determined to make Dakota say it. And finally, he did.

"You couldn't turn him into a vampire and save him?" Dakota asked.

"No." Paolo had lived with that guilt ever since his brother's death. "He was ambushed in the morning. I didn't know. I couldn't step out into sunlight. Had I known... I'd have done anything to save him, but for all that I'm this thing that scares you, I could do nothing to help him. Nothing." He opened his eyes and looked at Dakota. "I'm not all-powerful. I'm just me."

"What's going to happen to me?" Dakota asked after another moment of silence.

Paolo wouldn't lie to him. "Claude will arrive, and he'll decide whether or not to wipe away all memories and knowledge you have of vampires existing. Then he'll let you go."

Dakota sat up, looking startled. "Back to my brother, who'll want to know where I was last night?" Then his expression shifted to anger. "Hey, wait a freakin' minute! He's going to mess with my mind? That's bullshit! My memories are my own. He can't wipe them out! And how would I even know if he screwed up some other stuff in here?" Dakota tapped his temple. "No. No way."

"He won't give you a choice," Paolo said.

"So he'll rape me? Isn't that what it is, just mental?" Dakota's voice carried enough frost in it to chill the desert. "He'll dip into my brain against my will?"

"It's not like that," Paolo protested.

Dakota came to his knees on the bed. "The hell it's not! It's *my* brain, *my* memories!"

The door opened. "It *is* invasive," Erin chimed in. "But it beats being killed to keep vampires safe."

"Your argument sucks balls," Dakota retorted.

"And to think, I was going to make you pancakes. It's toast and badly scrambled eggs for you." Erin shut the door.

"He can't cook," Paolo said after a minute or so. "Be glad he's not making pancakes. Andrew, his twin, always talks about how crappy Erin's cooking attempts turn out."

"You don't know that yourself?" Dakota asked.

"Can't eat," Paolo informed him. "Some vamps can nibble here and there. I can't. Even a lick of food can make me feel queasy. I can sip water, though, and pineapple juice. Just those two things, though."

Dakota moved closer to the edge of the bed, by where Paolo was sitting. "How'd you figure that out?"

"Trial and error." Paolo imagined the food he'd grown up on. "I miss food. That was almost as hard to lose as sunlight, and being able to see myself in the river. I haven't seen my reflection since I was turned."

"I can't imagine that." Dakota was almost close enough to touch. "Paolo, I don't want my head screwed with."

"Only mates can know of us," Paolo started to explain.

Dakota pointed at the door. "Erin's someone's mate? And what do you mean by mate, anyway?"

"A mate is the human a vampire falls in love with, and vice versa." He might have been romanticizing it, but to him, that was what mates were. "Once they have committed to each other, a vampire will never feed from any other human. In return for sharing his or her blood with a vampire mate, the human's life will be extended to however long the vamp lives."

"How long is that?" Dakota asked.

Paolo wished Dakota would touch him. "Could be hundreds of years. Vamps possibly have eternal lives if someone doesn't murder them."

"Possibly?"

"No one is certain, because vampires get killed by cults that think it's fun to murder them," Paolo explained. "Or we screw up, get caught out in sunlight, something like that."

Dakota leaned down, lowering his elbows to his knees. He was so close, yet Paolo didn't dare touch him. "The… The human doesn't turn into a vampire?"

"Oh, no," Paolo replied, loosening his hold on his knees, and daring to hope that Dakota wasn't going to hate him.

"A vampire can't have another vampire as a mate. We can't...survive without human blood. We never turn our mates."

"Huh." Dakota gestured to the bed. "No coffins?"

"Only for kicks." Paolo knew how morbid that sounded, but it was true. "Some vamps like all the clichés, since most of them are true for us anyway. No sunlight, holy water, stakes, garlic, we turn into bats—"

"Bats?" Dakota frowned. "There was a bat last night, out by the porch."

Paolo nodded. "Jude. You met him at the club last night, when he was asking about being our third. I don't think he meant it, though, more like he was trying to help us escape. He was there to keep an eye on the Slayers as a whole."

"And what were you there for?" Dakota stood up, arms folded across his chest, and stared down at him.

"To see what was going on with new recruits," Paolo said bluntly. "And before you think I set out to seduce you, no, I didn't. The idea of sex with a Slayer or Slayer-to-be is repugnant to me. But you... You—" *Be honest. Just be honest.* "You are sexy and sweet, that's why I called you sugar. You didn't want to join the Slayers, and I just couldn't leave you to that fate. I wanted—want—to help you."

Dakota groaned and tipped his head up. Paolo watched the way his Adam's apple bobbed.

"I like you," Paolo added. "And I loved having sex with you."

Dakota made a frustrated sound as he flopped onto the bed, lying on his back. "I *suck* at this, at being able to tell when someone's full of shit, and why am I not more freaked out over this? Learning that vampires exist, and you're one, and I had sex with you and it was the best sex ever?"

Paolo seemed to perk up at that, no longer hunching over. "It was? Really? The best sex ever?"

"That's what you pick up on?" Dakota asked.

"I didn't even have to bite you to make it the best sex ever," Paolo mused. "Geez, I wonder how good it'd be if I *did* bite you?"

"No biting. None." Dakota sounded firm on that.

There was something Paolo couldn't help but notice, however. "You didn't say no sex."

Dakota groaned again. "Aw, God! I can't even say that and mean it. What'd you do to me?"

"You fucked me into bliss, sugar." The endearment slipped out before Paolo could censor it. "If it matters, it was the best sex I can remember having, too." And he'd had lots of sex, although not in the past few years.

"You didn't—" Dakota sat up and looked Paolo in the eyes. "You didn't mess with my brain, like that Claude guy can do?"

"Oh, no. I'm not a coven leader, and I'll never be as powerful as Claude. I don't want to be, either. I just want to be happy." That might be asking too much. Paolo didn't want to think so. "The Dark Slayers have hunted vampires for centuries. Maybe there was a need for that hundreds of years ago, but we've evolved as a species. We know we aren't demons or spawns of Satan, things brought up from the bowels of Hell. We don't kill our enemies, or else we could have wiped out the Slayers that are here in Vegas, at the very least. Claude made some of them forget about us, but he didn't kill any of them. Can't say the same for them."

"What do you mean?" Dakota asked.

Paolo had to change position. His lower back was starting to cramp. He stretched out his legs and lay back on the scratchy rug. "They've killed off members. That's all I know. You'd have to get the details from Claude."

"I don't think I want to talk to Claude." Dakota surprised him by nudging Paolo with one foot. "I don't want him messing with my head, Paolo. Help me avoid that."

As much as Paolo hated to, he had to deny that request. "I can't go against my coven leader's will. I am bound to him through blood and honor." The idea of letting Dakota down left a bitter taste in Paolo's mouth. "I'll talk to him though, I promise I will." He wanted to suggest that, if

Dakota was willing to date him, Claude might not interfere with his memories, although Claude would make rules. Probably lots of rules, most of which would involve Dakota staying at the vamps' coven in the desert, and far away from any Dark Slayers. That seemed like coercion to Paolo, so he didn't mention it.

He was tired, and worried. Paolo rubbed at his eyes. "What are you going to do?"

"Erin's not letting me out of this house, is he?" Dakota asked.

"No, he won't. He won't put his brother at risk. I'm sorry." And Paolo was sorry for that, though he was still glad he'd gotten Dakota away from the Slayers.

"His brother must be a lot better than mine," Dakota muttered. "Utah's a jerk. It's his fault I'm in this mess. No, wait. It's not. I made the decision to come to Vegas. I should have left as soon as he started in with the crazy talk. I just… wanted to belong. The money would have been nice, but it wasn't everything."

Dakota could belong with the vamps and their mates. The idea took root in Paolo's head and wouldn't be squashed. A vamp could and often did choose a mate quickly. Time was of the essence when a human could expose vamps to the world and end them, so it wasn't unusual for vamps to decide on a mate and woo them—sometimes in a matter of hours.

"What will you do now?" Had he asked that already? Gods, he was so tired. Paolo closed his eyes and thought about drifting off to sleep. There was nothing he could do right now that would help Dakota.

"I don't know. Maybe have a silent meltdown over all of this." Dakota didn't sound as if he were joking.

Paolo wasn't the type of person who sat around feeling glum. He was cheery and unencumbered by chronic worry. A couple of deep breaths was all it took to restore some of his hopeful nature.

He probably couldn't do much to help Dakota with

Claude, but he *could* offer him a distraction.

Suddenly, Paolo wasn't quite so exhausted. He grinned, glad to be back on familiar ground with himself. "Well, for now, do you want to fuck me again?"

Chapter Ten

Call him crazy, but Dakota most definitely did want to fuck Paolo again. He wanted to shut off his mind and fears and lose himself in sex. Dakota sat up and looked at Paolo. He didn't resemble the creepy movie vampires in any way at all. In fact, he looked more human than some people Dakota had seen, definitely more human than the hulking Jude from the night before.

Paolo was short, compact, not too muscled and with just a hint of definition to his abs. His legs were thick but not bulging. He had almost flat feet, the soles of which were pink, contrasting beautifully with the rest of his tanned skin. His toes were stubby, and Dakota had the strangest urge to suck on them. "I never had a foot fetish before."

Paolo smiled broadly, and opened one eye. "Yeah? You can have whatever kind of fetish with me you want, sugar, as long as it involves your mouth on some part of me. I'll be happy to return the favor."

Dakota had to be a ripe idiot, because he was seriously considering taking Paolo up on that offer.

"We don't need to use condoms, either, if you don't want to," Paolo added. "I'm, er, well—"

"I get it." The reminder of what Paolo was should have deterred him, yet Dakota was able to ignore it, because when it came down to it, the fact was, he wanted Paolo. Wanted to do so many things with him, to him. He examined the urge to do those things, and concluded that it wasn't desperation or loneliness driving him to accept Paolo's offer. It was just Paolo himself—sexy, giving, smiling at him like Dakota was someone special. Even being bad at reading people, Dakota couldn't miss that. Paolo all but glowed with happiness when he smiled at Dakota like that.

"I'll roll over, stay on my stomach," Paolo offered.

Dakota frowned as he tried to figure out why.

Paolo pointed to his teeth, which were now just plain teeth. "So you don't worry that I'll bite you."

Dakota snorted. "Right, because I didn't see you zoom across this room like some kind of naked superhero. You were a blur, Paolo. If you can move that fast, you being on your stomach won't ensure I don't get bit." He took a steadying breath, then forged on, because he was horny, Paolo was the sexiest man he'd ever get a chance to be with, and Paolo made him feel good when Dakota didn't think about the vampire bit.

And if there was a chance he was going to be forced to forget Paolo, he wanted to try to counter that, to maybe see if he couldn't embed a part of Paolo in his memory that no creepy Claude could remove.

Dakota slid down to the floor. Paolo's breath hitched and he opened his other eye when Dakota picked up Paolo's left foot.

Gaze locked with Paolo's, Dakota brought his foot up and licked at the smallest toe. He felt a little embarrassed at first, but Paolo gasped, twitched his toe, and grabbed at the rug.

"That feels good," Paolo said a moment later. "Didn't know— No one's ever done that."

Dakota liked being the first to do something to—with— Paolo. He didn't want to even think about how many sexual partners Paolo must have had in his past. If he went there, he might feel...less than up to the task, just from sheer intimidation.

So he shut out everything but Paolo, the taste and feel of him, the scent of him, the way Paolo's skin felt under his hands, under his tongue. Dakota stripped away his own inhibitions, knowing he might never have a chance to be so free with someone.

And he trusted Paolo, which maybe was crazy, or stupid,

or both. It didn't matter. When he looked at Paolo, instead of being afraid, he simply wanted him.

Dakota held Paolo's foot and kissed his toes, caressed Paolo's calf and admired the smooth musculature there. He rubbed the pad of Paolo's foot, and every time he pushed just so, Paolo would moan and twist his hips.

He was working his way up to Paolo's ankle when the sound of a doorbell ringing startled him and Paolo both.

"What the hell?" Dakota said as he let go of Paolo's foot. "Is Erin expecting company?"

"I don't know." Paolo shot to his feet, his hard cock slapping against his belly. "Shit! Your brother's here with some other people!"

"How can you —?" Dakota began.

Paolo tapped one ear. "Very acute hearing. I would have picked up on it sooner but you were melting me into a puddle of sexual bliss." He ran to the door and flipped several interior locks that Dakota hadn't noticed before. Then he began to unflip them. "No, I can't leave Erin out there alone!"

"You can't go out there either," Dakota said. "What's Erin saying?"

Paolo cocked his head toward the door. "He's refusing to let them in."

"Utah and the other Slayers? Or just Utah and who?" Dakota asked, coming to stand by Paolo.

"There are several of them — Slayers," Paolo said grimly. "Including your voodoo man. I suspect that's how they found you. Blood is a powerful magic."

Dakota supposed it must be, if it kept vampires alive. "They'll find you. You have to stay in here."

"I can't!" Paolo reached for the last lock.

Dakota grabbed him and tugged him away from the door. "Please, don't. Let me go out there. I'll tell him you're gone. That we had sex and you split on me."

"They might kill you, Dakota," Paolo said, his dark eyes so serious. "If they suspect even a little that you aren't on their side."

Shouts rang out, and Erin yelled, "What the hell did you just throw at my door? Get off the porch and leave or I'll call the police!"

"And we'll report you for kidnapping my brother," Utah shouted. "Try it, you vamp lover!"

Paolo jerked out of his grasp.

Dakota caught him again. "Don't," he said, not bothering to hide the urgency in his voice, the rawness of his emotion. "Please. Please don't go out there. Give me a chance to try to...to...make them go away. If I go out there, the might hurt me, but if you go out there, they definitely will kill you. They carry holy water and stakes and some new kind of stuff they call powdered sunshine that's supposed to cause a great deal of pain before killing. Please." He'd get down on his knees and beg if he had to.

Paolo went perfectly still in his arms. "They have that kind of technology? They've tested it?"

"So they say." Dakota shook his head. "I imagine they aren't lying. I thought they were full of shit, but vampires exist, and Ken, he was bragging about capturing a vampire in Texas and trying out the powder on her. He laughed when he talked about her screams."

"And yet we're the monsters," Paolo said, the words dripping with bitterness.

"I know. I know, so let me try to get them out of here," Dakota urged.

"They've been to this house before, a few years ago. Claude erased those memories, but what if this brings them back?" Paolo asked. "I don't know if that's possible, but it might be. Erin and Andrew recovered their memories through hypnosis."

"Okay, but we can't go rushing in there without a plan. If we do, that'll look suspicious, and Erin might get hurt," Dakota pointed out. "Think about it—the two of us, or even one of us, running out screaming at them to stop. That's confrontational, too, and it won't help Erin or us."

There was a loud bang, then Erin bellowed, "I'm calling the police!"

"Oh shit!" Dakota shoved Paolo away from him as hard as he could. "Stay here! Please!" Then he unlocked the door.

Paolo was on him in less than a second. "No! You can't do this!"

Dakota saw fangs, and it startled him. He still didn't back down. "You won't hurt me." And God, he hoped he was right about that. "You won't," he reiterated. "Let me go help Erin, and if he calls the cops, I can tell them I'm here of my own free will and that the Slayers are crazy as fuck. Just give me a chance to help you."

Paolo's fangs receded and he slumped against Dakota. "Fine, but if they hurt you or Erin, I'm coming for them."

Dakota figured that was the best agreement he'd get from Paolo on the matter. "Okay, and maybe you can do that bat thing and hide somewhere in here, in case Utah or Ken insist on checking the room?"

Paolo nodded once, then Dakota cupped his chin and kissed him before leaving Paolo alone. He just hoped that he could convince Utah and the others that they were way off track.

Dakota strode down the hall and grimaced as he heard Erin cursing and the sounds of fighting growing louder. Dakota ran the rest of the way, not stopping until he was prying Utah's hands off of Erin's throat. "What the fuck is wrong with you?" Dakota screamed at him. "Let him go!"

Erin's face was red, and he was weakly pummeling Utah's chest. The other Slayers were closing in.

"He's just a human," Dakota snapped. He drew back one fist and did something he'd wanted to do for weeks— punched Utah in the face.

And it hurt like fuck!

Utah let go of Erin and several Slayers surged toward Dakota, but Kellan stepped in front of him. "Cut this shit out," Kellan ordered. "We aren't murderers. This guy clearly isn't a vampire, so stop trying to kill him."

"But he's sheltering them!" Utah bellowed.

"You're crazy as fuck!" Dakota told him, peering around Kellan. "Vampires don't exist. All of you are crazy!"

Kellan turned and dumped powder on Dakota.

Dakota spluttered.

"He's not a vampire, either," Kellan pointed out. "So far, all we've found here is two humans."

"We haven't searched the place," Ernest said, narrowing his eyes and shaking a finger at Kellan. "Whose side are you on anyway?"

"The side that doesn't end up with me going to prison," Kellan snarled. "That means I won't let you kill innocent people."

"They aren't innocent," Ernest argued. "They're vampire lovers!"

"Oh please," Erin rasped from where he'd dropped to his knees on the floor. "I'm a psychiatrist. I'll be happy to charge you a small fortune to help shed your delusions."

"I'll call the police myself," Kellan warned.

"Do you know what we do to traitors?" Ernest asked, taking a step toward Kellan. He pulled a stake from his inside jacket pocket. "One guess. You'll be buried with the other fuckers that turned on us. The desert will take care of you then."

"You've really killed people?" Dakota was horrified, terrified, and possibly some other –fieds he couldn't think of just then.

"Oh yeah, and it was fun," Ernest informed him. "Nothing like getting rid of trash."

Dakota searched out his brother's gaze. "Utah, don't let this happen."

Utah shrugged, though he did look mildly uncomfortable. "He's our leader. Ken said there's at least one vampire here. We have to do what we have to do."

"And that means killing people because a crazy voodoo guy says so?" Dakota couldn't believe he'd almost let himself get pushed into joining a group of sociopaths! "No.

Not happening."

"Dad would roll over in his grave if he could see you." Utah sneered. "Can't blame him."

"Well, since he didn't bother to see me after I was ten, tough shit." Dakota glanced at Kellan and tried to figure out if he was an asset or not. "This is the last time I'll tell you— Vampires aren't real, and you aren't hurting Erin or me. Now, leave."

Ken the creeper cursed. "You have been defiled by the monster!"

"De—" Dakota couldn't help it, he laughed despite the danger of the Slayers. "Defiled? Jesus, what kind of crap is that? Defiled! I had sex with a man, and it was fantastic. Are you just jealous?"

"I have seen them," Ken snapped. "Killed them with my own hands and powers. Vampires are real, and you have consorted with them. I have your blood—"

"So who's the vampire then?" Erin asked, arching one eyebrow as he looked at Ken. "You're fucking bent, man. And is that some poor animal's pelt you're wearing on your chest?"

Ken was extremely hairy, and the open leather vest showed that.

"You think your wit will save you, but it won't," Ken threatened, taking a step toward Erin. "Kill him, Ernest. Leave that one"—he gestured to Dakota—"to his brother."

"What about the vampires?" Utah asked, and while he didn't argue over his task, he had turned a sickly shade of gray.

"We will take care of them after these two are eliminated." Ken's smile sent a shiver down Dakota's spine.

"There's no such thing as vampires," Dakota tried again. He and Erin were outnumbered, and even if Kellan helped them, he doubted they would defeat the Slayers.

Dakota glanced at Kellan, who was completely expressionless. Erin scrambled over to Dakota's side, and Dakota helped him to his feet. "Stay behind me, Erin."

"I can fight," Erin rasped. "I really can. I knew what I was doing."

"Seriously?" Dakota was certain he was supposed to be reading some hint in Erin's eyes or face, something, but he just wasn't getting it. "You still—"

Someone shoved the front door all the way open, letting the sunlight stream into the room.

"Wouldn't want some vampires coming out from the rest of the house and trying to rescue you," Ernest said, smirking as he took a second stake from his jacket. "No mercy, Slayers, just like the vampires would do to us. Kill 'em!"

Chapter Eleven

Paolo heard the order to kill, and he reached for the door. He didn't know what he was going to do, exactly, but he couldn't stay in there and let innocent people get hurt, or killed.

He opened the door just a crack, and let himself change into his bat form. He slipped out of the room and stopped as soon as he saw the sunlight streaming in. It reached the start of the hallway, and that meant he'd turn to ash quickly if he went very far.

"You don't want to do this," someone said from the living room.

"Kellan, you're supposed to be one of us. I am very disappointed in you. I hand-picked you, but I guess even the leader of the Slayers can make mistakes."

Paolo was guessing the first speaker was Kellan, the second was Ernest. He slapped a little closer, trying to figure out how he could help.

He saw Kellan reach into his vest.

"Stop him!" Ernest shouted.

Dakota yelled, possibly a war cry, though it sounded like he'd stubbed his toe. "Bring it!"

Erin spun and kicked — and Kellan held up something in his left hand while pointing a very large gun at Ernest with the other. "Drop the stakes! *Now!*"

"You're a cop?" Dakota asked, and he wasn't the only one with that question.

"Shit! We can't kill a cop," Utah said, backing away. "That's a death-penalty offense."

"Not if the body's never found." Ernest didn't move any

closer to Kellan, despite his words.

"I'm wearing a wire," Kellan said with a definite *duh, you dummies* tone.

"Then we're already fucked," Ernest retorted. He roared and ran at Kellan.

Half the Slayers went barreling out of the door, but the other half stayed, surging forward and bellowing as they attacked.

Kellan started shooting. People began to scream in pain, and Dakota as well as Erin were fighting for their lives.

And Paolo couldn't help them.

Or can I? He flapped a couple of times as he considered his options, then he transformed and strode closer to the light. "Looking for me?"

Dakota tried to whirl around but his brother had him in a headlock. "Paol— Urgh!"

"Come fight me like the badass you think you are," Paolo said, baring his fangs, letting his vamp out. "Come on, cowards!"

Kellan had been tackled by several men. His gun wasn't in his hands. Erin was martial-artsing his way through Slayers as fast as he could. Dakota...was stuck in that headlock. Paolo hissed and looked right at the voodoo man. He knew the voice, had heard it from the bedroom. *Ken. What the fuck kind of voodoo priest name is that?*

There was nothing mystical or magical about the man, Paolo knew it in an instant. Whatever Ken's game, he was a liar.

They had found Dakota somehow, though. Paolo would worry about that later. For now, he pointed at Ken and gave him the one-finger, come hither signal. "You and me, asshole."

Ken raised his arm, and Paolo knew what he was going to do before it happened.

Paolo shot up the wall and onto the ceiling, clinging like a spider as the powder Dakota had warned him about scattered over where he'd been standing. A few sprinkles hit his back, and the pain was indescribable. Paolo refused to make a sound. He scrambled along the ceiling, then dropped down once he was past the dust. He was almost to the sunlight.

Dakota shouted and desperation showed in his movements as he finally slipped from his brother's hold. "Jerk!" He punched Utah low, landing the blow almost at his groin.

Utah turned white and fell to his knees, howling until he vomited.

Dakota dashed over to the door and slammed it shut.

Erin took down a Slayer with a kick to the head.

Paolo shot forward and tackled Ken before he could throw anything else. He could only imagine how insane he looked himself—naked, eyes red, fangs showing.

Well, he wasn't a monster. He could have ripped Ken's throat out, but settled for a pulled punch to his temple. Full strength would have crushed Ken's skull.

As it was, Ken would be unconscious for a while.

Paolo leaped up and was immediately faced with another Slayer. "You want some of this?" Paolo licked one fang.

"N-no," the Slayer stuttered, eyes huge. "No!"

Paolo shoved him down. "Stay put, or else."

Then he grabbed one of the men trying to kill Kellan. "Enough!" He shook the man hard before tossing him aside. "Stop this!"

Kellan was either dead or unconscious. Paolo focused on him and heard an unsteady heartbeat.

Paolo roared, more for effect, because he'd long ago learned that a roaring vampire was frightening to humans. That sent most of the ones on Kellan running, and Erin, along with Dakota, took care of them while Paolo rolled Kellan to his back. "Oh…shit." Blood flowed from a wound on Kellan's chest. "Call an ambulance!"

And where was Ernest? Paolo spotted him stooping to pick up the gun by the edge of the couch.

Paolo was going to become Ernest's worst nightmare—a

naked, pissed-off creature of the night. He moved as fast as he could, evading the bullet fired at him, and slapped the gun out of Ernest's hands. Dakota dove for it and grabbed the weapon.

"No one is going to believe you," Paolo said as he swung behind Ernest. "Rant all you want about vampires. It'll just get you more meds where you're going."

"Fuck you," Ernest retorted. "Pussy, that's what you are!"

Paolo wasn't offended. That was a lame insult, plus he could smell Ernest's fear. "Say goodnight, Ernest."

"You'd better fight—"

Paolo was done fighting idiots. He hit Ernest hard enough to shut him up, and let him fall to the floor. A quick check and he saw that all the Slayers had either fled or were incapacitated.

"I've called nine-one-one," Erin said, wiping blood off his cheek. "I don't know if Kellan will live long enough for an ambulance. Could you—"

"No." Paolo cut the question off. "I can't. I really can't. I gave a vow to Claude. I don't think I have the ability to turn him, either." Not all vamps could. Paolo had never tried. He'd never wanted to turn someone into a vampire, to take away their sunlight.

Erin's pinched look darkened to anger. "Then get a hold of Claude! Have Abernathy bring him, or something."

It would take Claude too long to get there since the sun was out, but Paolo didn't say as much.

"I'll call Abernathy now. Do you want me to call Andrew, too?" Paolo asked.

"Yeah." Erin didn't look away from Kellan.

"Dakota, is everyone incapacitated?" Paolo thought so, but it never hurt to check. He started looking for the landline, but the handset was off the base. "Erin, where's your cell phone?"

"Was on the table, I think."

"Everyone's down and out," Dakota informed him. "I don't know for how long though."

"Hopefully as long as we need them to be." Paolo didn't see the phone on the table, no surprise since someone had managed to knock it over. He knelt and looked under the chairs and cabinets, then saw the phone under the microwave cart. Paolo retrieved it and stood just as the wail of sirens rent the air.

Paolo rushed from the kitchen into the living room. "The police—"

"I'm not mentioning you at all," Dakota vowed. "Go. Hide. Make those calls, quickly, if you have to make them."

"Dakota—"

"Go," Dakota snapped, not looking at him.

It was unreasonable to feel hurt, or as hurt as Paolo did then. He'd disgusted Dakota so much the man wouldn't even glance his way.

Paolo started for the dark bedroom and saw the powder spread over much of the hall floor. If he hadn't had the phone, he'd just have gone batty and flapped over the caustic crap. His back began to burn again, or he became aware of it again, Paolo didn't know which. He heard the sirens—they were quite loud, probably half a block away— and knew he had to do something or get ashed when the front door opened.

Paolo couldn't cling to the ceiling without both hands. He wasn't talented like that, and he preferred to have his feet on the ground, or floor. His choices were limited by a substance he knew would kill him. In a moment of desperation, he backed up, then sprinted forward and leaped. His left heel landed in some of the powder and the pain shot up to his hip. Paolo stumbled the rest of the way into the dark bedroom, then spent a few minutes typing out a message to Abernathy, who could pass the information on to Andrew. Once he sent it, Paolo turned the phone off. Abernathy wouldn't respond, since Paolo had told him not to.

Ignoring the pain from his wounds, Paolo wiped down the phone then left it on the nightstand. He morphed into a bat and flapped around for a moment before landing on the floor. He tried not to worry about how mad Claude would be—another human, possibly two, left to run around all willy-nilly, with knowledge of vampires.

As Paolo waddled under the bed, it dawned on him that he didn't know where Dakota had lived with Utah, or how to get a hold of Dakota. Before he could do anything about that, he heard the arrival of emergency crews, ambulances and police.

He'd have to hope that he could find Dakota. The cops would clear the house out, mark it off as a crime scene.

Somehow, he'd find Dakota again.

Chapter Twelve

"Scars are sexy," Radney said. "That's what you told me about the holy water ones."

Paolo tried to peer over his shoulder at the scars. He could feel the small spots, the skin puckered up like pebbles, mementos of the night before. "I wish I could see myself in a mirror."

"Well, you can't, so take my word for it. Claude healed you up pretty nicely." Radney touched one of the spots.

"I sure wish we knew what that shit was," Andrew said. "Those scars are— Er. I mean, they look like something is under them, you know."

"Yeah." Paolo glanced down at his foot. The heel was pebbled with marks from the powder. "No one's going to want to lick that foot."

"Gross, dude, no. No foot licking," Radney protested, shaking his head. "Ew."

"You've licked my feet before," Andrew pointed out. "And just last week, you masturbated—"

Radney waved his hands at Andrew. "No! You can't tell anyone about that!"

"This calls for a toe jam joke somehow, I just know it."

Paolo grinned at that, turning to find Augustin entering the room.

Radney groaned and hung his head in a show of dejection. "Augustin. Of course you'd have to hear that."

Augstin grinned wickedly. "Oh yeah. There will be much gossiping and joking about jam in the kitchen soon."

Radney huffed and looked sideways at Augustin. "Really? Can't you move past what I did?"

"Oh, honey, I moved past that long ago," Augustin informed him. "Now I just torment you for fun, not revenge. Kinda like I do everyone else. You're one of Uncle Augustin's special people."

Andrew walked over to Augustin. "Hey, don't you have your own mate to pick on? Or some poor bug's wings to pluck off?"

"Ew, that's nasty! I don't touch bugs, not even to smush them." Augustin shuddered. "That's Tony's job, but he's doing some drill with Claude," Augustin replied. "Drill, schmill. There's only one thing he needs to be drilling." He slapped his generously proportioned rump—*no one* called Augustin a fat ass anymore, not since the hot sauce incident. "Anyway, Clod wants you to come chat with him in his office in an hour. I guess he's doing the whole kingly leader of the vampires shit tonight, sending me to deliver a message like I'm some...some gofer or whatever."

"Were you doing something else?" Andrew asked. "Or were you bugging Claude while he was doing whatever drill with Tony?"

"You know what, fuck you, Mr. Logic." Augustin grinned though, which meant he was not irritated with Andrew. "Yes I was. I was following them and asking Clod why he thought it was necessary to take away my valuable sex time with Tony. Then I started asking him how Abbie felt about not getting any. Hence—*tada!*—here I am."

Paolo had watched the whole mock-bickerfest with amusement, though he was nervous about the meeting with Claude. It wasn't often Claude sent for him. Most of the time, if Claude wanted something from Paolo, he simply showed up wherever Paolo was. Sometimes, that didn't afford them any privacy.

"Your scars look hot," Augustin said. "You're going to be getting laid like crazy now."

"I think he's got the sweets for someone," Radney teased, waggling his eyebrows at Paolo.

Paolo plastered on a grin despite the butterflies in his

stomach. "Maybe. If I can find him."

"Can't believe you let your guy get away without getting any contact info from him." Augustin tutted. "I thought I raised you better."

"Apparently not," Paolo countered. "Anyway, I need to get dressed."

"Eeee, that's a shitty diversion of topic," Augustin muttered. "Is this a broken heart deal?"

Paolo laughed at that. "We fucked once, and knew each other for maybe twelve hours, tops. Not enough time for broken hearts." Just maybe enough time for his heart to kind of decide it really, *really* liked Dakota. "And he probably won't want to see me ever again after all the crap that went down."

"Yeah, Erin still can't go back to the house," Andrew offered. "Which he has bitched about to no end. Claude's going to have a cleaning crew go over there as soon as the cops give the all-clear. Until then, I think Erin's camping out at the Bellagio."

"*Camping out* at the Bellagio?" Augustin sniffed. "Right. It's the freakin' Bellagio. No one *camps out* there. I am *so* jealous."

Andrew looked askance at him. "That's not even the nicest hotel in Vegas."

Augustin widened his eyes. "Heresy! You'll burn in hell for that, you heathen."

"I'm terrified," Andrew replied. "I will admit that the fountains there are my favorite thing on the strip."

"Not the people handing out all the titty cards?" Radney asked. "I keep waiting to get handed some dick cards, but it's always about women—come see our naked women at this club, or this one, or this one. Jeez, sometimes I think there are more naked women in Vegas than clothed ones. We need to make that happen with men. Nudity for all."

"Oh, really?" Andrew asked.

Radney nodded. "Yeah, sure, because then you'd like going to the Strip more. You like ogling naked men."

"I like ogling *one* naked man," Andrew corrected.

"Me?" Radney nodded. "Right. Me."

"You two are entirely too syrupy in love," Augustin griped. "I'm leaving before I get cavities." He left the room without a backwards glance.

Andrew, Radney and Paolo looked at each other.

"Well, at least he didn't get too snarky with any of us this time," Andrew surmised. His phone buzzed and he took it from his pocket. He read the message then sighed. "Erin just got back from the hospital after checking on Kellan Eddings. Turns out he is a cop, but he was on personal leave, so that means he was infiltrating the Dark Slayers on his own. If he ever wakes up out of the coma, maybe he can tell us why."

"Does it matter? As long as he lives, that's what's important," Paolo pointed out. "Now shoo, and let me have some peace before I have to meet with Clod. Claude. *Claude*, damn it."

Radney and Andrew laughed as they left his room.

Paolo sat on the bed and stared down at his scarred heel. Now that he was alone, he just wanted to think about Dakota. Paolo thought they'd really had a connection, maybe even the potential to be mates. He was jumping the gun on that, but he couldn't help it. It was in his nature as a vampire to move fast on a mate, and everything with Dakota had felt right. At least, Paolo had thought it did. Dakota might have had a different opinion, and he *had* seemed angry or dismissive, or both, the last time he'd spoken to Paolo.

"I'm a happy guy," Paolo reminded himself. "And I have a fantastic butt." *And scars that should have healed up completely. What was in that powder that even Claude's blood couldn't heal them?*

Paolo would have to deal with the scars. Maybe it wasn't such a bad thing that he couldn't see his reflection after all. He wondered if Dakota would have sympathy sex with him because of them. He'd rather that Dakota just want him, but he wouldn't turn down a sympathy fuck from him

94

if that was the most he could get.

Because he wanted Dakota, and no one else. The man was right for him, and he'd do whatever he had to do in order to be right for Dakota.

As long as Dakota could love a vampire. Paolo didn't expect roses and a wedding band, or vows of never-ending love—yet. But someday, he wanted all of those things with Dakota.

Sitting around moping wasn't going to get him his man. Paolo got up and kicked off his tattered sweats. He put on his best jeans, the ones that really emphasized his…assets, and a cute green T-shirt with a giggling dinosaur on the front of it. A pair of flip-flops, and he was dressed. He fussed with his hair until it was almost time to meet Claude, then he left his room and went to join the coven leader.

Claude was already sitting behind his desk, looking very lord of the manor-ly. He had on—as always—an expensive designer suit. This one was in a light gray, the material somewhat shiny. He wore a lavender shirt under it, and a tie that blended perfectly with the outfit.

"Do you ever have a hair out of place and totally freak out?" Paolo asked after he'd been told to enter.

Claude smiled. "No. Now have a seat, and let me tell you what I have learned about the Slayers and Dakota Dickens. I was very unhappy about him escaping before I could make certain he wouldn't cause us harm." He folded his hands together neatly on top of the desk.

Paolo was never going to be that calm, composed and cool.

"A little investigating has led to the information that the Dark Slayers are done here," Claude began. "While Kellan Eddings wasn't on a case, he did record the entire encounter at Erin's, and every meeting he had with the Slayers, including his private 'friend' times with Utah. I'm not certain of the legalities there, but on top of that, several of the Slayers admitted to murderous acts or knowing of murderous acts once the police began interviewing them.

Bodies have already been found in the desert, so I believe this will put an end to the Slayers here, as I said. I am also uncertain as to why Kellan was involved, though if I were to hazard a guess, it would be that the Slayers had harmed someone he cared about."

"That would make sense." Paolo leaned forward in his seat. "It's funny, when I saw him at the club, I thought he was different. His tattoo looked off."

"It wasn't a real tattoo. Erin has asked me to turn him, if he doesn't improve," Claude said. "I prefer to do no such thing. Just as I prefer not to let humans run around knowing about us. To that end, I am going to have to deal with Dakota."

"Deal with him? How?" Paolo shook his head. "I know how. He just pointed out to me that by going into his head, you're violating him."

Claude scowled. "I—"

It was the first time Paolo had seen him flustered. "I don't think anyone would believe him," Paolo offered. "If he decided to tell. Did any of the police officers believe the Slayers?"

"To my understanding, no. They believe the Slayers to be an unstable cult." Claude's expression evened out. "I think I understand what Dakota means. It is a very fine line that I walk in trying to protect this coven. I will always do what I must to keep it safe."

"I understand," Paolo murmured, even though he hated the idea of Dakota's memories being erased.

"Paolo."

Paolo raised his gaze to Claude's. "Yes, sire?"

"Does he mean something to you?" Claude asked.

Paolo hesitated to answer as he tried to decide what he felt. After a minute, he thought he knew. "I like him, a lot, and I think he could mean something to me. We don't know each other, but there was a connection there. Unless... unless I broke it when I went all vampire on the Slayers. Then, maybe, I scared him, or disgusted him."

"Or he might have been overwhelmed by the violence and his own brother trying to kill him," Claude surmised. "I suppose you should talk to him and see if you and he can reach some sort of agreement."

"Agreement?" Paolo felt the seed of hope in him bloom into something much sturdier. "You mean, you won't make him forget me? Us?"

"Only if it's absolutely necessary," Claude replied. "I like to believe myself an intelligent and fair man, and a progressive one as well. Perhaps I should have a little more faith in humans, and in my coven members' choices in potential mates. That *is* what we have been talking around in regards to you and Dakota, is it not?"

Paolo nodded. "It is, but I don't know—" He was so nervous! "How do you know when you've found the one who should be your mate?"

"There is no sure way of knowing. Look at what happened with Abernathy. He was mated to a vampire who almost killed him just to break the bond between them. Had I not found Abernathy when I did, and had he and I not admitted our feelings for each other, I would not be alive, sitting here with you tonight." Claude smiled. "If you think this man is worth it, then take a chance on him. There will be rules, of course."

"Of course."

Claude was being more generous with Paolo than he'd been with other vamps when they'd fallen for their mate.

"Don't look so surprised, Paolo," Claude said quietly. "I have favored you since I found you so long ago. Had you shown any desire to lead…"

Paolo was deeply touched, and very glad Claude knew him well. "No, not me. I wasn't a leader when I was human, and that hasn't changed. I just want to be happy, and loved."

Claude stood. "You are loved, but I think perhaps you mean a different kind of love. To that end, come with me."

Paolo didn't ask any questions. He followed Claude, and nourished the hope that was still growing.

Chapter Thirteen

Dakota looked at the hulking man on the motorcycle. "Are you kidding me?"

"Nope. Get on." Jude held a helmet out to him. "We're going to be late."

Dakota took the helmet and silently called himself a fool as he put it on. There he was, getting on a motorcycle with a vampire. His life couldn't get any stranger.

But it might get better than it'd ever been. He got on the motorcycle and wrapped his arms around Jude as much as he could. They took off, rocks spitting out from behind them. At least, Dakota thought that was the case. It sure seemed like Jude had gone from zero to sixty in under ten seconds, which would have sent pebbles flying.

Or it was entirely possible that Jude wasn't going that fast, and Dakota was just scared shitless because he'd never ridden a motorcycle before. And he was doing that with a gigantic vampire.

Who was taking him to meet up with Paolo.

Dakota's heart pounded. A couple of feet below, something else had blood pounding into it. Dakota willed his burgeoning erection away. Then he noticed the vibration from the bike. He gave up on not getting a hard-on and thought about Paolo.

Most of those thoughts were X-rated and damned entertaining on the ride.

When Jude slowed the bike and turned down a dirt road, Dakota tried to figure out where they were. It was dark except for where the headlight spanned out. The moon, when it was visible, was just a sliver, and clouds covered most of the stars.

They bumped along the dirt road for what felt like miles before Jude turned again, this time into a driveway. He shut the motorcycle off.

Dakota let go of him and got off the bike. His legs felt a little shaky. He unfastened the helmet and handed it to Jude. "Thanks."

"No problem." Jude stowed the helmet. "You hear that buzzing? That's the buggy."

Dakota heard it, the drone of an engine coming closer and closer. He took a few steps in the direction the sound came from. He was so eager to see Paolo, and maybe he shouldn't have been. Dakota discounted that thought. Though he hadn't spent much time with Paolo, he felt like they'd made a connection. Dakota wanted to explore that.

He watched as twin headlights appeared over a dune. They were on the edge of the desert. Dakota waved, even though he couldn't tell if Paolo saw him. The idea of meeting Claude scared Dakota, but he was going to do it. He glanced back at Jude. That big hulker was going to put a rut in Dakota's plans to fight Claude off if Claude tried to fuck with his head.

The buggy drew closer, then closer still until it was a dozen feet away. The sight of Paolo caused a bit of chaos in Dakota's body. He wanted Paolo, badly.

The refined-looking man with the perfect hair and wearing a very nice-looking suit with *had* to be Claude.

Dakota turned his attention back to Paolo. It was hard not to run over to him— Then Dakota asked himself why he was holding back. Paolo was smiling at him. Dakota could see the white flash of his teeth even with the headlights on behind Paolo.

There was no reason not to be honest about the way he felt. Dakota told himself to dive in or walk away.

He dove, jogging over to Paolo. "You're okay." He cupped Paolo's cheek. I saw you step in that powder but I was afraid to go after you. Didn't want to lead the cops to you."

"I have scars," Paolo said, staring at him. "On my back, and my foot."

Dakota leaned closer, slipping his other hand around to Paolo's back. "I'll kiss every one of them," he whispered in Paolo's ear. "Every inch of you."

"Well, it seems that Dakota has retained an interest in you." Claude's droll tone eased some of Dakota's fear of the vampire. He sounded like he wasn't about to jump on Dakota and screw with his memories.

Paolo slid his arms around Dakota and pressed in close to him, resting his head on Dakota's chest. "Mm. So does that mean he and I can have some privacy to talk?"

"Talk, is it?" Claude chuckled. The man was stunning, physically perfect, yet he didn't appeal to Dakota at all. "First, let me introduce myself. I am Claude, coven leader and friend of Paolo." Claude extended his right hand to Dakota.

Dakota had to stop touching Paolo's cheek so he could shake Claude's hand. "Dakota Dickens, but I guess you know that since you sent Jude to find me."

"Actually, I had you found before that," Claude informed him. "Erin saw you at the hospital."

"I wanted to make sure Kellan was okay. He's not." Dakota swallowed back the nausea he felt making his jaw tingle. "He looks bad."

Claude nodded once. "So I have been told."

"Can you help him?" Dakota asked.

Rather than answer, Claude gestured Jude over. "Please keep an eye on Kellan at night."

"I will." Jude gave Dakota and Paolo a two-fingered wave. "Later." Then he left them with Claude.

Claude waited until the motorcycle was out of sight before he spoke again. His gaze seemed to drill right through Dakota's, as if Claude could see into his thoughts.

"Don't," Dakota snapped. "None of that!"

"I was merely looking at you, Dakota," Claude said. "I

was not putting you in thrall."

"Uh huh." Dakota wasn't sure he bought that line.

"It is the truth. Paolo told me you were ardently against me altering your memories—which, by the way, is how I believe Ken found you at Erin's." Claude tipped his chin toward Dakota. "He hypnotized members of the Slayers and found the ones I had blocked memories from. That is my supposition. I have learned that blocking memories is not a foolproof thing, which leaves me with trusting someone—you, specifically, because Paolo cares for you, and I care for him as his sire."

"Sire?" Dakota repeated.

"I did not turn him, which is what a sire is—the vampire that turns a human," Claude explained. "However, once I found him, I gave him my protection, my blood, and my affection. I suppose I am more of an adopted sire."

"No, you're just my sire," Paolo said. "And my friend."

"Good." Claude smiled again. "As I said, Paolo likes you. He hopes that together, you and he might have the kind of relationship that all vampires crave. If you cannot let Paolo bite you, feed from you, however, then Paolo's hopes must be set aside. So tell me, Dakota Dickens, can you handle a vampire's bite?"

Could he? Dakota was not big on pain. In fact, he didn't like it at all. "Um, how often would you need to…to do that?" he asked of Paolo.

"Every few days," Paolo replied.

"Though it feels very good to both parties, and it is not unusual for mated pairs to do it on a daily basis," Claude informed him. "It depends on how much blood Paolo would take. A small amount daily, a sip, if you would. Whatever works for you and him. I will stress that, as lenient as I am being, I am also putting a limit on the amount of time you two have to decide whether or not you are suited as mates."

"We've only just met," Dakota argued. "How can we know how well we'll be together unless we spend months—?"

"Weeks," Claude interrupted. "Four, to be exact, and I

feel I am being generous. This is a non-negotiable period of time."

"And if I don't agree because I want more time?" Dakota pushed back at Claude's rule. "Or if we end up not working out?"

"Won't happen," Paolo murmured, his breath warming Dakota's skin through his shirt.

"Then," Claude drawled, "I will deal with you as I see fit."

"*That's* not a threat at all," Dakota said.

Claude hummed while tapping his chin with one finger. "All right, I won't kill you, or clear your memories. I want you and Paolo to have this time together without pressure that it must work or else I'll do something. Three weeks it is."

"Three—" Dakota scowled at Claude. "You said four weeks at first!"

Claude shrugged, and his grin wasn't a very nice one. "I changed my mind." And from one second to the next, he was gone.

Dakota blinked, then blinked again and looked at Paolo. "How did he do that?"

"He's Claude." That was the only answer Paolo gave him.

"Well, okay then." Dakota tipped Paolo's chin up. "I really want this to work."

Paolo licked his lips and Dakota's erection was back in action, filling out quickly.

"So do I," Paolo admitted. "I thought you were angry at me when you sent me to the room."

"Angry at you?" Dakota replayed that moment in his head. "Oh. I did come off as snappy. I was just trying to get you to safety, and trying to wrap my head around having my own brother try to choke me to death. That disturbed me like nothing else."

"I'm sorry he hurt you," Paolo said. "Physically, yes, but emotionally too. You need family."

"I wanted him to be family, but he wasn't, not really.

Family doesn't turn on you like that." Dakota brushed his lips over Paolo's. "I can live without him."

Paolo's bright smile warmed Dakota's coldest places, the parts of him that were wounded by family, by a rotten ex who'd broken his heart.

"I want you to come back to the coven house with me," Paolo surprised him by saying. "You need family. Come see what my family is like, what you can be a part of, if we suit each other."

Dakota wanted that, the dream Paolo was offering him. "Okay. Take me to your home."

Epilogue

"Mm, honey, you have a nice ass on you," Augustin said. "Better get it into the kitchen and get your mate before he starts talking to Andrew. You'll never get Dakota alone if that happens."

Paolo hurried down the steps from the room he shared with Dakota. They'd been mates for almost two months and every day was better than the one before it, as far as Paolo was concerned. He hit the last step and turned around the banister—and pulled up short as Dakota came out of the kitchen. The smile on Dakota's face was the most beautiful thing Paolo had ever seen. "Hey."

Dakota winked at him. "Hey, yourself. You slept late. I was coming to get you up." He leered and Paolo's dick gave a happy twitch.

"How convenient," Paolo returned, eyeing his mate hungrily. "I was coming down for a bite to eat."

Dakota blushed, the scent of his arousal becoming pungent in the air. "Well, why are we standing here talking?"

Paolo laughed and grabbed Dakota's hand. "Come here."

Paolo had only meant it to be a quick kiss, but when his lips touched Dakota's, that electric jolt of lust they shared erupted and he thrust his tongue into Dakota's mouth.

Dakota began touching him everywhere, hands moving nonstop as he backed Paolo up.

Paolo's right heel hit the bottom stair. He had to end the kiss or risk falling. It was a near thing, because he wanted to keep kissing his mate. "Stairs," he whispered before grabbing one of Dakota's hands. "I'll race you!"

Dakota slapped Paolo's ass. "You're wearing a thong.

How am I supposed to concentrate on winning when all I can do is look at your gorgeous ass?"

Paolo laughed and started up the steps. "That's why I'll win, and winner gets to top."

"I'm all for that." Dakota trotted up the stairs behind Paolo. "You really do have a perfect butt, the globes plump but not too much so, soft padding with hard muscles underneath. And tight—your ass grips me like a clenched fist. Perfect."

"Aw, thanks, sugar, but I'm still fucking you," Paolo informed him.

Dakota liked to top most of the time, but on occasion, they both needed something different.

Dakota sighed as if he were always so put-upon. "Fine, if I *have* to, I'll let you put that thick cock of yours in my ass." They reached the top of the stairs and Dakota grabbed a double handful of Paolo's butt. "Sweet."

"Yours, sugar." Paolo loved being able to say that. "Now come on and kiss me."

Dakota turned Paolo around and kissed him, an aggressive surge of tongue and teeth, Paolo nipping at his lip, drawing a little blood.

Dakota moaned and shivered. He often said that if humans knew how orgasmic a vamp bite was, they'd be clamoring for them. Paolo knew that was the truth.

Paolo got them into their room, and Dakota stripped the thong off him immediately after he kicked the door shut.

"God, I want you in me so bad," Dakota panted. "Help me get naked."

That was code for *Rip my clothes off, I want it rough.* Paolo was happy to oblige. He tore Dakota's T-shirt down the middle then pushed it down his arms. The pajama bottoms were trickier. Paolo had them off in pieces with a few careful jerks.

Then he was kissing Dakota again, backing him up step by step, caressing Dakota's belly, his chest, his back, his ass—everywhere he could reach. When Dakota was close enough, Paolo gave him a push. He pounced on Dakota as soon as he hit the bed.

Paolo licked and nipped his way from Dakota's lips to his chin all while touching him. He tugged and pinched at Dakota's nipples, keeping the pressure to them light since they were so sensitive. "Sweet, sugar," he murmured, not caring if he was babbling. Dakota was filling him up, taking over his senses, so that all Paolo could believe in at that moment was his mate.

He dragged one fang over Dakota's sternum, then lapped at the tiny speck of blood that welled up.

"More," Dakota demanded. He wasn't a shy lover at all. "Now. Come on, Paolo!"

Paolo didn't answer except to drop more kisses and nibbles on Dakota, working his way down to the fat head of his cock. He pressed one fang to it, just letting Dakota feel, not threatening or promising. A bite there was possible, but not something they'd ever discussed.

Dakota's breath hitched. "Suck me, please, please!"

Paolo licked the head, tasted the bland pre-cum leaking from his slit. Then without warning, he took Dakota's full length into his mouth, his throat. He flicked his tongue all around, knowing every vein by heart. At the same time, he played with Dakota's balls, tugging, rolling, pressing them closer to Dakota's body.

Dakota moved his legs restlessly and grabbed at Paolo's hair. He began to thrust when Paolo bobbed back up to the top of Dakota's shaft, and together they moved, spiking pleasure higher with each second.

Paolo let the saliva run down from the root of Dakota's shaft, over his balls. He rubbed his fingers in it, then moved them back to Dakota's tight hole. When he pushed them into that gripping heat, Dakota howled like wolf calling the moon. He arched and shoved his ass down, trying to get more fingers, deeper.

Paolo thrust them into Dakota again and again, found Dakota's gland and gave it a touch.

"Fuck!" Dakota bellowed, legs spreading wider, ass going tight around Paolo's fingers.

Paolo sucked the crown of Dakota's cock and rubbed his gland again.

Dakota grunted and thrust hard, sinking his dick into Paolo's throat.

Paolo took the face-fucking eagerly, his own shaft so hard he ached. He pumped his fingers in and out of Dakota's hole until the outer ring had softened up enough for something bigger.

Then he stopped sucking Dakota and instead grabbed the lube. His hands shook as he opened it and poured some into one hand. He wanted, *needed* Dakota so bad.

And soon, he'd have him again.

Paolo pushed slick lube into Dakota's ass with his fingers, then added more and worked it inside of Dakota, wanting him good and wet. When Paolo's fingers slid in and out easily, he scooted into place and pulled his fingers free. "Love you, sugar," he said as he began to push his cock into Dakota's tight hole. "So much." God, the heat, the grip of that ring and those inner walls was going to melt Paolo someday.

"Love you too," Dakota rasped, grabbing at Paolo's shoulders. "Fuck. Me."

Paolo didn't need to be told twice. He thrust hard, sinking his cock into Dakota's ass, then pulled almost all the way out before doing it again.

He raked his fingertips over Dakota's chest, his shoulders, arms and hips, even his thighs, while he fucked him hard and fast.

Paolo's orgasm was building up fast, too fast. He wasn't going to last long.

"P-Paolo." Dakota arched, reaching for his shaft.

It was the signal Paolo had been waiting for. He rolled Dakota's ass up, folding him over enough that Paolo could reach the tender spot they both liked him to bite. As soon as he was able, he pressed his teeth to that sweet spot where

Dakota's neck and shoulder joined, and he bit.

There was nothing like the taste of Dakota—salty, sweet, hot, somewhat metallic. Paolo drank, savoring each drop of his mate's blood. It thrummed through his veins and bound him to Dakota even more, and Paolo craved that like nothing else.

Dakota went rigid under him, and his ass clamped down so tightly around Paolo's cock that he couldn't move it. He held still and let Dakota's rippling inner walls pull the climax right out of him. Paolo loved leaving his cum in his mate.

He shuddered as the last shot left his cock, then Paolo eased Dakota's legs down, helped him unfurl, all while keeping his shaft in Dakota's warmth.

Dakota sighed happily and wrapped his arms around Paolo. "Stay inside of me all night."

Paolo nodded. "Anything you want, sugar. Always."

And he meant it, and always would.

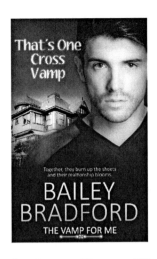

That's One Cross Vamp

Excerpt

Chapter One

Sunlight—Erin Meyers loved it. He rolled onto his stomach and tugged his ball-snugglers up so his tan line wouldn't show when he went to the beach wearing his bathing suit that made a Speedo look like a Puritan's modest dress. He had a nice ass, and when he was out prowling for men on the beach, he liked to go as close to naked as possible.

Erin sighed and drifted a little, letting himself completely and utterly relax. It'd been a bad week at the office. As a psychiatrist, he saw all sorts of people, but for the most part he managed their medications after meeting with the person one time. After that, he had them start therapy with a psychologist or licensed therapist. Sure, he saw those patients monthly for check-ins, but… Well, he made a shit-ton of money, but lately that just didn't seem to matter.

Kind of like getting laid wasn't the priority it'd once been.

God, he was closing in on middle age, depending on the average male life span in America. He wasn't going to look it up—he didn't need that kind of depressing info. He was going to be forty soon, though, and like the typical, clichéd guy in the throes of a mid-life crisis, Erin was finding himself dissatisfied with everything.

And having to work so much harder not to have parts droop or go to fat.

And he had gray hair at his temples, which he dyed religiously.

And he was getting ear hair. *What the hell is up with that? Like anyone needs the additional intrusion against being able to hear? Is that why so many elderly people are almost deaf? Overwhelming ear hair?*

Then there were the latest results of his physical and bloodwork. High cholesterol, plus some other questionable results that needed further research.

"No." Erin was going to relax, enjoy the sun, and not let anything ruin his day. He took half a Xanax, needing to bank the anxiety threatening to build rapidly. He picked up the Beats headphones he'd set by his lounge chair, connected them to his iPod, and put on his favorite playlist as loud as he could get it. Then he carefully blanked his mind, and after a while, dozed off under the hot Nevada sun.

* * * *

It's a damn good thing I'm burn-proof. Erin sat up, awakened, he guessed, by his playlist ending, or his Beats dying…or the iPod dying. When had he last charged either of those, anyway? Erin shrugged and stretched. He was drenched in sweat, warm through and through, and he felt great. That nap had been just what he needed before a night out.

His twin brother Andrew had long ago settled down with one man… *Okay, one vampire.* Erin had stopped being freaked out about the existence of vampires way back in his early twenties. Even then, when Andrew had stumbled upon their existence, Erin had been less surprised than he should have been, probably. Well, he'd always been the cynic out of the two of them, so it just hadn't blown his mind to discover human beings weren't the be-all and end-all of intelligent life forms.

He'd also been the shallower of the two. Andrew was the introvert, the loyal lover and mate. Erin was the bitchy playboy, although he kept the bitchy to an as-needed basis more often now.

Erin shook off his wandering thoughts. Andrew had always been a homebody and Erin had not, that was the gist of the whole thing, anyway. Erin was also aging, and Andrew was not—a benefit of being a vampire's mate.

More books from
Bailey Bradford

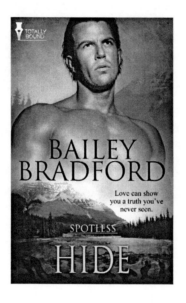

*When you think you'll never fit it, never be whole, love can
show you a truth you've never seen.*

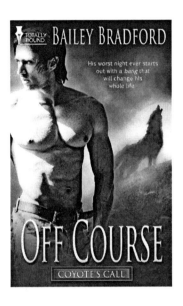

Gideon's worst night ever starts out with a bang that will change his whole life.

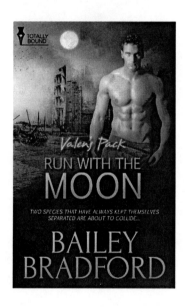

Two species that have always kept themselves separated are about to collide and create a new world.

A run through the woods turned anything but typical when Levi found the one thing he never expected to find— his mate.

About the Author

Bailey Bradford

A native Texan, Bailey spends her days spinning stories around in her head, which has contributed to more than one incident of tripping over her own feet. Evenings are reserved for pounding away at the keyboard, as are early morning hours. Sleep? Doesn't happen much. Writing is too much fun, and there are too many characters bouncing about, tapping on Bailey's brain demanding to be let out.

Caffeine and chocolate are permanent fixtures in Bailey's office and are never far from hand at any given time. Removing either of those necessities from Bailey's presence can result in what is known as A Very, Very Scary Bailey and is not advised under any circumstances.

Bailey Bradford loves to hear from readers. You can find contact information, website details and an author profile page at https://www.pride-publishing.com/

CPSIA information can be obtained
at www.ICGtesting.com
Printed in the USA
FSOW02n0951050716
22360FS